THE
RECKONING

Also by Wade Hudson

Defiant

THE
RECKONING

WADE HUDSON

CROWN BOOKS FOR YOUNG READERS
NEW YORK

Text copyright © 2024 by Wade Hudson
Jacket art copyright © 2024 by Jethro Unom

All rights reserved. Published in the United States by Crown Books for Young Readers, an imprint of Random House Children's Books, a division of Penguin Random House LLC, New York.

Crown and the colophon are registered trademarks of Penguin Random House LLC.

Visit us on the Web! rhcbooks.com

Educators and librarians, for a variety of teaching tools, visit us at RHTeachersLibrarians.com

Library of Congress Cataloging-in-Publication Data
Names: Hudson, Wade, author.
Title: The reckoning / Wade Hudson.
Description: First edition. | New York: Crown Books for Young Readers, 2024. | Audience: Ages 8–12. | Audience: Grades 4–6. | Summary: Twelve-year-old Lamar dreams of becoming a filmmaker, but when his grandfather is killed in a racist act of violence, Lamar becomes determined to honor his legacy by documenting the fight for justice.
Identifiers: LCCN 2023025759 (print) | LCCN 2023025760 (ebook) | ISBN 978-0-593-64777-6 (hardcover) | ISBN 978-0-593-64778-3 (library binding) | ISBN 978-0-593-64779-0 (ebook)
Subjects: CYAC: Race relations—Fiction. | Documentary films—Fiction. | Video recordings—Production and direction—Fiction. | Grandfathers—Fiction. | African Americans—Fiction. | LCGFT: Novels.
Classification: LCC PZ7.H868 Re 2024 (print) | LCC PZ7.H868 (ebook) | DDC [Fic]—dc23

The text of this book is set in 12.5-point Adobe Garamond Pro.
Interior design by Michelle Crowe
Grunge masking tape illustration: Bakai/stock.adobe.com

Printed in the United States of America
10 9 8 7 6 5 4 3 2 1
First Edition

Dedicated to all of those who are standing up for freedom, justice and fairness everywhere! The struggle must continue!!

CHAPTER 1

Lamar Phillips sat on the front steps of his house on Jones Street, just chilling, trying to decide what to do with his Saturday. He picked up his new video camcorder. Until Gramps helped him buy it, Lamar had been using his iPhone to record videos. He knew that an iPhone wasn't what real filmmakers used. Neither was a camcorder.

Lamar took it everywhere. He practiced recording slow motion, motion detection, time-lapse and self-shooting with it. He used it to interview students and to record football and baseball games at school. That is, when he was allowed to. Adults were always telling him to leave the premises. When he recorded a fire at a house in Morton, the firefighters asked him to move on because he was getting in their way.

One day, he reasoned, he would get a 16 mm camera, like the Panasonic AG-CX350 4K camcorder he saw in a magazine. It was a real professional camcorder. Lamar knew he could become a big-time director with a camera like that. It cost more than $4,000. That was a lot of money. So, for now, his video camcorder had to do.

Lamar held the camcorder up to check it out, to make sure everything was working right. Nothing had really changed since he last held it. The truth was, he just liked holding his first video camcorder. Lamar wanted to be a filmmaker. He had read books about the craft. He had watched as many movies and series as he could, on television, streaming and at the movie theater in Morton. He enjoyed all kinds of movies. Besides those that Spike Lee, his role model, had made, his favorites were those that featured superheroes like Miles Morales and Black Panther. He saw the first *Black Panther* movie *five* times. He had never before seen so many powerful Black characters on-screen together. Whenever he watched *Black Panther,* he discovered something new and exciting. When Chadwick Boseman, the actor who portrayed Black Panther in the movie, died, Lamar cried. It was like somebody in his family had died.

"What's up, Junior?"

Lamar looked up from the steps where he had been

sitting and saw his best friend, T.C., approaching. Always joking, T.C. had called Lamar a name he knew that Lamar didn't like.

"I've told you 'bout calling me Junior," Lamar scolded him. "You know I don't like it."

Named after his father, Lamar Eugene Phillips, Sr., Lamar didn't like Junior. He never used it unless he had to . . . like when his homeroom teacher made him add it when he turned in an assignment. Junior just didn't sound cool.

"I know you don't like it. That's why I call you that."

T.C. placed a hand on Lamar's shoulder and flashed that bashful smile for which he was known.

"I'm just messing with you, man!" he told him. "I'm just messing with you. Don't get all wired up."

"I ain't wired up. I just don't like to be called Junior, that's all. Hold this."

Lamar gave T.C. the cover to his video camcorder he had now placed on his lap. T.C. grabbed the cover and held it tightly.

"I'll just call you Spike since you're always talking 'bout him. That's cool, ain't it?"

"Spike's the man, T.C. You know that," Lamar said, revving up like a car engine at the start of a race. "He's been making movies since the 1980s. He's the GOAT.

Look at how many movies he's made. He did *Mo' Better Blues, Malcolm X, Jungle Fever, He Got Game, She's Gotta Have It.* Spike's bad!"

"You weren't even born when those movies came out," T.C. teased.

"So what? They're played on cable channels all the time. I don't miss one when it's on."

T.C. smiled again. He knew how to get his best friend started.

"You forgot *Do the Right Thing*," he interjected, still smiling. "I saw that movie three times with you when it came on the movie channel."

"I saw it four times. It's considered one of the best movies of all time," Lamar said flippantly. "See, T.C., I check out all these movies to study the techniques filmmakers use," he went on. "I study the craft like the books say you should do."

"Well, I like to be entertained," T.C. shot back.

"That's the difference between me and you. I'm serious about the career I want to pursue. Being serious means, you know, you gotta prepare. You got to study."

"Yeah, yeah, yeah. You go on and be Spike Lee," T.C. said, brushing off his friend. "I'm cool with being your assistant. Spike had help, didn't he?"

Lamar didn't say a word. He was now focused on his video camcorder. T.C. got the message.

"So, where're we going today?" he asked, changing the subject.

"I ain't got nothing planned. I'm just gonna let it roll," Lamar answered. "Since it's Saturday, we got most of the day to try to figure something out."

"Yeah. But what?"

T.C. sat on the steps next to Lamar. A brisk breeze blew a candy wrapper near their feet. Lamar picked it up and shoved it into his pants pocket.

I didn't pick up all the trash? he thought. *All I need now is for Mom and Dad to get on my case.*

Suddenly, T.C. snapped to attention and turned to face his friend.

"Let's go to that softball game they're playing this afternoon," he suggested excitedly. "We can video it. Your Pops playing, ain't he?"

"Naw. He went fishing," Lamar answered nonchalantly. "Anyway, we videotaped the game they played two weeks ago. Nothing ever happens in Morton. It's a boring country town."

Disappointed that he had no answer, Lamar leaped up from the steps, still holding his video camcorder.

"I gotta find something to videotape," he exclaimed. "Something that's interesting! How can I learn how to be a good filmmaker when there's hardly anything important to videotape?"

Lamar walked restlessly from his yard to the edge of the unpaved street.

"Interesting like what?" T.C. asked, catching up. He wasn't really expecting an answer. If there were something worth videotaping, they would have found it last week or the week before.

Lamar didn't answer. He walked a few aimless steps farther into the street.

Suddenly, T.C. perked up again.

"Why don't we go up on the Hill?" he offered. "Something is always happening on the Hill."

Lamar still didn't respond. Not knowing what else to do, T.C. picked up a small rock and threw it at the tall pine tree across the street. When the rock hit the tree dead center, Lamar jumped back, shocked.

How many times has T.C. missed that tree before? he thought. *How many times has T.C. missed hitting anything?*

But T.C.'s broad smile told Lamar that T.C. wasn't thinking about all the misses. He was enjoying his recent success.

"Like Steph Curry hitting a long three," he joked.

"Yeah! Big deal." Lamar shrugged. "Big deal."

"It is a big deal," T.C. said. "I nailed it. So, what do you think about my idea?" he asked again.

"I think I'll pass." Lamar answered quickly this time.

"Dad and Mom might find out about it. Your dad and mom, too. And we would be in big trouble."

The Hill was located in the south side of Morton where Lamar and T.C. lived. It was an area Lamar's parents had always told him to stay away from. The few nightclubs in the neighborhood were there, and several pool rooms, as well as other small businesses such as Miss Molly's Café.

"Remember that time me and Kyra went to Miss Molly's to buy some of her famous fruitcake?" Lamar reminded T.C. "I thought Dad and Mom were gonna ground us forever."

"Why people think the Hill's so dangerous?"

"Because they always fighting up there, T.C. Something bad is always happening there. Somebody got shot there some time ago. Remember?"

"Yeah, I remember. But ain't nothing gonna happen on a Saturday morning. Besides, if you stay here, you just gonna be videotaping people walking the streets or driving by in their cars. What's exciting about that? We don't have to go inside the nightclubs or Miss Molly's. Ain't hardly anybody on the Hill during the daytime, anyway. We can just walk around a little. It's no telling what we might see that we can videotape."

Lamar walked away from his best friend, not wanting to hear any more.

"You're just tryin' to get us in trouble, T.C."

"Naw, I ain't, Lamar," T.C. continued, following his friend. "We ain't gonna get in no trouble. We can just keep on walking. We don't have to stop. You wanna get something different to videotape, don't you?"

"Yeah, but . . ."

"Aw, Lamar. You ain't chicken, are you? You ain't afraid?"

"I'm supposed to fall for that, T.C.?" Lamar retorted.

"Fall for what?" T.C. responded coyly, as if he wasn't aware that he had struck a nerve.

"I'm supposed to go to the Hill to prove I ain't scared? Gimme a break, T.C.! You know me better than that."

Lamar moved a few steps away again and began filming with his video camcorder.

"You're wasting time now, Lamar," T.C. told him. "You ain't recording anything worthwhile. Just trees and stuff like that." Frustrated, T.C. threw another rock at the tree. This time he missed.

"When we get there, we're gonna walk past, right?" Lamar asked, thinking more seriously about T.C.'s suggestion. "We ain't gonna stop?"

"Naw, we ain't gonna stop," T.C. answered, now pumped up because of Lamar's sudden interest. "I told you that!"

Lamar thought he would try it. He was determined to find something worth videotaping.

CHAPTER 2

On the way, Lamar kept thinking about what would happen if his father and mother found out they had gone to the Hill. Why had he allowed T.C. to talk him into going? But each step they took brought them closer to their destination.

"What's up, dudes?" A loud voice caught Lamar's and T.C.'s attention.

They turned around to see Philyaw Henderson, the high school basketball phenom, jogging up to them. He caught T.C. on the head with a playful slap.

"Come on, Phil," T.C. complained, rubbing the stinging area. "That hurt." Philyaw just laughed.

"Don't be soft, dude. What're you knuckleheads up to, anyway?"

No one knew why he was named Philyaw. Some said

his mother was trying to be creative. Though odd, the name didn't bother Philyaw. Lamar had interviewed him when he first got his video camcorder. That was the only significant interview he'd had. Philyaw had been interviewed by television and newspaper reporters because he was big news—the best basketball player in the entire state of Louisiana.

"Is Kyra home?" Philyaw asked Lamar. "I wanna drop by to see her."

Phil stared at Lamar hopefully.

"Yeah, she was there when I left," Lamar answered. "On that computer of hers as usual."

"Oh, man. I better not bother her then. I know how she is when she's doing schoolwork. One of those college scouts is coming by my house in a little while. I'm ducking out. I think I've had about twenty-five come to interview me and check me out over the last semester. It can get tiring, man."

"You've probably already made your choice?" Lamar asked.

"I've narrowed the list down. That's for sure."

"You a superstar, Phil," T.C. said, laying it on. "Man, I would be eatin' up all that attention."

"It would wear you out, lil' brother, believe me."

Phil fist-bumped Lamar and T.C. and walked away, his long legs making giant strides.

"Ol' Phil will be in the NBA very soon," T.C. told Lamar. "He only has to go to college for one year and then he can go to the NBA. Man, Phil is Magic, LeBron and Michael Jordan all rolled into one. I wish I was him."

"You can be successful, too, T.C.," Lamar told his friend as they continued walking to the Hill. "You don't have to be envious of other people. Me, I'm gonna be a big-time filmmaker. Just wait and see. You just gotta find what *you* wanna do. You know, what *you* enthusiastic about."

"I'm not good at much," T.C. complained in a tone that sounded like self-pity to Lamar. "I'm not good at sports or singing, stuff like that."

"Stop being so negative, T.C.," Lamar chided. "Everybody is good at something. You just gotta find what it is."

"How do you do that? How did you decide you wanted to be a filmmaker? I mean, I always knew you wanted to be one. But when did you *know*?"

"I've always wanted to make movies," Lamar shared. "Ever since I was a little kid. I used to watch movies, even when I was, like, six and seven. Remember when you used to wanna go play, and I would be watching something on TV? I would be dreaming. Dreaming that one day I could make a movie like that. You would get mad at me 'cause you wanted to play. Then I read about Spike Lee and all the movies he made. That's when I knew for sure I wanted to be a filmmaker."

"I remember those times you talkin' 'bout. I would have to be by myself. Playing by yourself is boring."

Lamar stopped and turned to face T.C.

"I don't know, T.C. Some people find out early in life what they wanna be. I guess that's me. Listen, you like messing with mechanical things and stuff like that, don't you? Maybe you can be an engineer."

"An engineer?!" T.C.'s face brightened. "Now, what exactly does an engineer do?"

"There are different kinds of engineers, T.C.," Lamar answered. "There's mechanical, electrical, civil engineers." Lamar saw the confused look on T.C.'s face. "We can Google it."

"Yeah. Let's do that. I wanna know more about that."

"We'll check it out," Lamar assured him. He knew T.C. was serious because he wouldn't normally agree to anything that had to do with spending time doing research.

When Lamar and T.C. reached the Hill, they stopped and stared at the small buildings before them. Lamar looked at T.C. and T.C. looked at Lamar uncertainly.

The Hill wasn't a big area, just four short blocks on Jefferson Street with buildings on both sides. It had been a part of the south side of Morton for a long time. The establishments were built close to each other with little space between them. Folks who owned them did their best to make them look nice, keeping them freshly painted with bright colors that made the entire area stand out.

"You ready?" T.C. asked Lamar nervously.

"Yeah, I'm ready," Lamar responded in a soft voice. They then moved slowly up Jefferson Street. Miss Molly's Café, the first place they reached, was painted dark blue with a light blue awning that had *Miss Molly's* written on it in bold white letters.

"Everybody says Miss Molly makes the best-tasting cakes and pies," T.C. told Lamar. "And other dishes," T.C. added.

"I know that, T.C. But my mother can burn, too," Lamar shot back. "Miss Molly got to do a lot of good cooking to out-cook my mom. I like her fruitcake, though."

The two friends stood in the street. From a distance, they could see several couples seated at tables inside.

"Not much there to videotape," Lamar commented under his breath. So, he and T.C. continued to walk up the street. Romero's Pool Hall, the only building painted white, was the next business they reached.

"A lot of guys go there to shoot pool," T.C. shared offhandedly.

"They go there to watch football and basketball games on that big television, too," Lamar added.

"How do you know?" T.C. asked. "You been in there?"

"No!" Lamar answered quickly. "You know I ain't been in there, T.C. I heard guys talkin' 'bout it at school."

"I didn't think so."

As they moved on, Lamar and T.C. heard music coming from the Red Room. It wasn't noon yet. But no matter what time of day, someone was always in the Red Room listening and stepping to the music.

"That's where that guy got shot, ain't it?" T.C. asked.

"It was Miss Bertha's son. I think his name was Tyrone." Lamar and T.C. checked out the place.

"I can see why it's called the Red Room," T.C. said, laughing. "It's red as a Santa Claus suit."

The outside *was* painted all red, but the front door was gold, like it was the entrance to a special place. After making sure no cars were coming, Lamar stepped farther into the street, raised his video camcorder and began videotaping the front entrance of the club.

Suddenly, a dark-skinned man and a tall, thin lady wearing a sky-blue dress walked out. Embracing each other, they headed toward Lamar.

"I look good, don't I?" bragged the lady, slurring her words. She pulled away from the man and began to strut as if she were a model walking the runway at a fashion show.

"Can I get a copy of those pictures you're taking?" she asked Lamar.

"I'm not taking pictures," Lamar responded, his video camcorder still rolling. "I'm videotaping. You don't mind, do you?"

"No, I don't mind. What you wanna be? A reporter or something?"

"No, ma'am. I wanna be a filmmaker."

"A filmmaker? Like Spike Lee? I love me some Spike Lee. He's kinda cute with his short self."

The man with her gave the lady a quick pull to move her along. She got the message.

"Well, good luck, honey. I'd go see your movies. Morton needs somebody famous to put it on the map."

The couple walked away, each measuring every step. But that didn't prevent them from staggering.

"You got that?" T.C. asked, smiling. "She's funny."

"I sure did," Lamar answered, smiling too.

"I think they're both a little drunk."

"More than a little, T.C."

Continuing to videotape, Lamar turned his video camcorder toward the buildings across the street. Out the corner of his eye, he saw a short, muscle-bound man with a thick mustache and a neatly trimmed beard walk up behind him. Wearing a yellow fedora, a dark blue suit and a white shirt but no tie, the man seemed out of place for an early Saturday morning.

"What're you doing, youngblood?" the man growled at Lamar.

As soon as Lamar got a good look at him, he recognized who he was. Everyone in Morton knew Mike Crosby. If you wanted liquor, a gun or drugs, Mike Crosby was the man to see. He had a crew that worked for him, some of whom were students at Morton Middle School and Morton High School. For anything that's illegal, Mike Crosby was the one to see. He had been in jail more times than anyone could count. But he always seemed to beat the charges.

"What're you doing up here with that camera?" he asked Lamar. "What're you recording for?" The stern expression on his face alarmed Lamar. Mike looked as if he was ready to snatch Lamar's camcorder from him.

"I'm just doing a little videotaping, that's all," Lamar told him, backing farther into the street. T.C. had moved even farther away, and it had been *his* idea to go to the Hill.

"What for?!" Mike Crosby responded.

"What for?" Lamar repeated the question, turning away from his inquisitor, who was now standing menacingly in front of him.

"Am I hearing an echo?!" Mike Crosby shouted. "Yeah,

that's what I asked! What for?" He took a step closer to Lamar.

It's obvious this dude ain't joking around, Lamar thought. He could see the fury on Mike's face. Lamar was so scared he couldn't think of a response.

Mike Crosby continued with his grilling. "I'm going to ask you again. What're you filming up here for?"

Lamar had to come up with some kind of answer, fast. But what could he tell Mike Crosby that would cool off the tough guy?

"I'm doing a documentary about the town," he muttered, some of his words incoherent. He continued anyway. "I wanna get footage of some of the businesses on the Hill."

That was the best he could do as he stood trembling, clutching his video camcorder in his hand.

"That don't fly with me, dude!" Mike Crosby came back at him. "You understand what I'm saying?"

Mike Crosby clenched his right hand into a fist and moved closer to Lamar, almost nose to nose.

"This is my office, and I don't want anybody videotaping, filming or whatever, where I do business!" he yelled out, words and spit shooting from his mouth. "Who sent you here with that camera?"

Lamar stepped away from Mike Crosby's hot, alcoholic breath, readying himself for the man's next move.

"We're leaving, Big Mike!" T.C. finally spoke up, hoping that would help to placate the town gangster. "We're leaving!"

T.C. walked away but stopped to see if his declaration had worked. Lamar started to leave, too, but Mike Crosby stepped in front of him.

"What you already got on that camera?!" he demanded. "I wanna see what you got. You probably got me on there."

Mike Crosby reached for the camcorder, but Lamar jerked it from his grasp. The town's tough guy grabbed one of Lamar's arms.

"Let me go," Lamar pleaded, trying to pull away. "I didn't record you! I didn't record you!"

"Lamar! Lamar!!!"

The voice sounded so loud it seemed that it had come from a megaphone. It got everyone's attention. Even Mike Crosby's. Lamar looked to see from where the booming voice had come. Across the street, he saw his grandfather getting out of his old blue Chevrolet.

"Come here, Lamar," his grandfather called loudly.

Mike Crosby loosened his hold on Lamar. As soon as he did, Lamar ran as fast as he could. So did T.C. After reaching his grandfather, Lamar looked back to see if Mike Crosby was following.

Mike seemed as if he was about to charge. Instead he just stood there, fuming.

"What are y'all doing up here?" Lamar's grandfather yelled at him and T.C. "You know your parents don't want y'all up here. And what y'all doing talking with that character? He's nothing but a gangster. Get in the car. I'm taking y'all home."

Lamar and T.C. slid quickly into the back seat. Mike Crosby had disappeared when Lamar glanced back to see where he was. Lamar stared at T.C. For once, T.C. didn't have anything to say. He knew his suggestion hadn't been a good one.

"One of y'all get in the front seat," Lamar's grandfather chided them. "I ain't no chauffeur."

Lamar eased out of the back seat and sat in the front next to his grandfather. He knew he had a stern lecture coming. He needed a reason to explain why he had gone to the Hill.

"Now, can y'all tell me why you came up here?" his grandfather asked.

"Gramps, we was just walking, and I started video-taping a little. That's why we was here. Mike Crosby came walking up. We didn't say anything to him."

"What did he want? He ain't nothing but trouble."

Lamar placed his video camcorder next to him.

"Gramps, the truth is, I just wanted to shoot something exciting, something important, with the video camcorder you helped me buy. So T.C. suggested that we go to the Hill. We didn't go to hang around or anything like that. We were just gonna walk past it, that's all. And that's the truth."

"Yet and still, you shouldn't be up here," Gramps scolded his grandson. "Y'all know better. There ain't no excuses. Too many bad things happen here. If your parents find out about this, y'all would be in big trouble. So, we won't let them know if you promise me y'all won't come here again."

"We promise," Lamar and T.C. answered in unison.

It was quiet as Lamar's grandfather's car made its way slowly down Jefferson Street. Lamar breathed deeply. He knew something bad could have happened to them.

"You want something exciting to videotape?" Gramps asked, looking over at Lamar. "Come with me to the town council meeting on Tuesday evening. There'll be plenty of excitement there. I'm gonna raise hell 'bout these streets still not being paved. And I ain't leaving until I get an answer."

"We can go?" Lamar asked excitedly, happy that Gramps had changed the subject. "Me and T.C.?"

"Yeah, you and T.C. can go," Gramps answered. "And they better not mess with y'all either."

Lamar reached back and slapped five with T.C. Then he leaned his head comfortably on the headrest. The Mike Crosby incident was in the past, and he wanted to leave it there. Tuesday evening was now on his mind. Finally, he would have something important to videotape. He couldn't wait.

CHAPTER 3

"Come on. We better hurry," Lamar told T.C. as they made their way to school. "Mr. Deloria closes the door if you get to school late. We got a long day, you know. We're going to that council meeting tonight, remember."

"I didn't forget," T.C. responded, running to catch up. "How could I? You been talkin' 'bout it every day since your grandfather told you to come."

"We've been waiting for something important to videotape, ain't we?"

"I know. I know."

When Lamar and T.C. reached Morton Middle School, they saw Frankie Pierce and Jimmy Clay standing at the bottom of the steps to the school building. Much bigger than Lamar and T.C., Frankie and Jimmy were two of the troublemakers, bullying other students, skipping class and playing pranks. Both had repeated several grades.

Lamar and T.C. started up the steps to the building, but Jimmy rushed over to block their way, smirking as if he had accomplished something important. Every time Lamar and T.C. tried to walk around him, Jimmy got in their way.

"Y'all gonna be late," Frankie said, falling to his knees in laughter.

"Where's that video camera, Spike Lee?" Jimmy teased Lamar, encouraged by Frankie's applause. "You got it hid somewhere?"

"You know I can't take my camcorder to school. Come on, Jimmy, you gonna make us late. Let us by," Lamar said quietly, not wanting to make a bigger issue out of something so trivial. He knew Jimmy was trying to bait him.

"*Make* me move!" Jimmy demanded. "If you're so bad, make me."

Jimmy pointed a finger in Lamar's face and Lamar knocked it away.

"You gonna get it now, boy," Jimmy barked at Lamar, making a fist as he moved forward.

"What's going on here?"

It was Mr. Deloria, the principal.

"Why aren't you in your classes?" Mr. Deloria stood with his arms folded.

Jimmy and Frankie snapped to attention. Lamar and T.C. relaxed.

Busted, Jimmy moved so Lamar and T.C. could pass.

Smiling with relief, Lamar and T.C. hurried inside. Jimmy and Frankie followed, walking slowly as Mr. Deloria watched their every step. Their smiles had disappeared.

Language Arts was Lamar's favorite class at Morton. And Ms. Harper, who taught it, was his favorite teacher. When the unit on drama began, Lamar could barely wait for class to start. He loved learning everything related to writing, about character development and motivation, the elements of a plot, and dialogue. A filmmaker needed to know how to write well.

"You have a good imagination," Ms. Harper told Lamar one day in class. "But you need to work on your writing skills."

So, Lamar had begun to write, sometimes poetry, other times short stories. When Ms. Harper told him his writing skills had improved, Lamar felt thrilled.

━━ ━ ━

Lamar and T.C. didn't take any classes together, except Physical Education. But they always ate lunch with each other.

The cafeteria at Morton Middle School was where

everyone could discover who hung out with whom. The athletes sat together. The smart students did, too. So did the girls who thought they were cute, the cool kids, and the troublemakers like Jimmy and Frankie. And the White students sat with each other, too, the few who attended Morton.

The noise was loud when Lamar entered. After waiting in a long food line, he placed a hamburger, French fries, a cup of Jell-O, a slice of cheesecake and a carton of milk onto a tray. When he spotted the table where he usually sat, he saw Jefferson Wilson, one of the White students at Morton, sitting alone. Jefferson wanted to be a filmmaker, too. That was how he and Lamar had struck up a friendship.

"What's up?" Lamar greeted Jeff as he placed his tray on the table.

"You, bro," Jeff answered.

Lamar thought "bro" sounded funny coming from Jeff, but he had gotten used to it now. It was better than "partner," which was what Jeff called him when they first met.

"I saw another Bogey movie last night," Jeff told Lamar, smiling proudly.

"Yeah? Which one this time?"

Beaming, Jeff answered, "*The Treasure of the Sierra Madre*. Walter Huston was in it. His son, John Huston, directed it."

"That's the one where they go prospecting in Mexico,

isn't it?" Lamar asked. "Bogey, the old man and another younger man?"

"Yeah. Tim Holt played the younger man. Bogey was awesome in that movie."

"To you, Bogey was awesome in every movie he did."

"Well, he was. Bogey was the best. No one was as good as Humphrey Bogart. Not Jimmy Stewart, Henry Fonda, Spencer Tracy or Cary Grant. Bogey was cool, but he was a great actor, too. No one played tough guys better than him. And he was versatile. He could do comedies, westerns and gangster roles."

"What about Denzel Washington or Chadwick Boseman?" Lamar asked jokingly.

Jeff looked up at him and smiled. "Not even Denzel Washington or Chadwick Boseman. But they're both great actors, too."

"Jeff, why you so into old movies?" Lamar asked. He had wondered why before but hadn't approached Jeff about it.

"My grandfather," Jeff responded.

"Your grandfather?"

"Yeah. He wanted to be an actor when he was young, but it didn't work out. When he moved in with us, that's all he would do, watch old movies. I used to watch them with him. He would tell me all about the actors and the directors. So I became a fan, too."

"I'm gonna learn about the history of Black movies and Black actors," Lamar said. "You know so much about White movies. I ordered this book called *Smoketown: The Untold Story of the Other Great Black Renaissance*. It's all about Black movies back in the day. I can't wait for it to get here so I can start reading it. I'm gonna know as much about old Black movies as you know about White movies."

"Why you call them White movies?" Jeff asked, looking side-eyed at Lamar.

"Because that's what they were," Lamar answered quickly. "Weren't hardly any Black people in those movies. Weren't no Black people in *The Treasure of the Sierra Madre*, was there? When there was Black people in those old movies, they played maids or butlers."

"Hamburgers again!"

Ciara Butler, a neighborhood friend of Lamar's, interrupted them, setting her tray on the table across from Lamar. Following her closely, T.C. placed his tray on the table, too.

"What are you looking at?" Ciara barked at Lamar, after catching him staring at her.

"You," answered Lamar. "You must have got your hair done last night."

"So? What's it to you?"

"It looks good, that's all. You look good in braids."

"My aunt did them. I got tired of having my hair straight."

"You do look kinda cute, Ciara," T.C. chimed in, unable to hide the smile on his face.

"Who asked you?" Ciara chirped back at him. She grabbed the hamburger from her plate, took a bite and then bit down on a French fry.

"Did you tell Jeff about the videotaping you did on the Hill?" T.C. asked Lamar, changing the subject. T.C. started wolfing down his food while still eyeing his friends' plates to see how much they were going to eat.

"You're so gross," Ciara told T.C. as he took a giant bite from the hamburger.

"That was a bust, T.C. You know that," Lamar responded to T.C.'s question.

"What's the Hill?" Jeff wanted to know.

"It's nothing, really," Lamar answered. "It's that part of town where we live that has clubs, pool rooms and other stuff like that. We were gonna videotape there, but we ran into this old gangsta dude who hangs out around there."

"When are you going to videotape *me*?" Ciara piped up while she pushed the remainder of her hamburger aside and slid the cheesecake in front of her.

"Ciara, I've been asking to videotape you ever since I got my camcorder. You always say no."

"I wasn't ready," she answered. "I am now. I got my hair done. I'll let you know when. Okay?"

"Just call me," Lamar replied. Knowing he was waiting for it, he gave T.C. his cheesecake. Lamar was no longer hungry. Ciara had made his day.

"You don't sit with us anymore, huh, Jeff?"

The sudden appearance of three White students startled them. Cap, the one who had spoken, glared at Jeff. An eighth grader and a member of the baseball team, he was the leader of the group.

"What do you mean?" Jeff asked innocently.

"You don't want to be with us anymore!" Cap bit down on his bottom lip. "Ain't it obvious? You ditched us!"

"I didn't ditch anybody," Jeff protested defiantly. "I sit with you guys sometimes, and sometimes I sit with other people. What's wrong with that?"

Cap shook his head, brushing Jeff off like he was flicking away an annoying fly. He and the other two stormed off.

"The nerve of those guys," Lamar said to no one in particular. "Who do they think they are? They think they own you or something?" he asked Jeff.

Shaken by the incident, Jeff kept quiet.

"Are you losing some of your friends by sitting with us?" Ciara joked flippantly.

Jeff still didn't answer.

Ciara picked up her tray and walked away.

"I have choir rehearsal," she said.

"Don't forget, we have to set a date for me to videotape you," Lamar reminded her.

"I told you, I'll call you when I'm ready," she replied. Then she was gone.

Lamar, T.C. and Jeff continued to sit at the table. None of them were in a hurry to get to their next class. The cafeteria was half-full now.

"Jeff, you ain't worried 'bout those obnoxious dudes, are you?" Lamar asked, seeing the agitated look on his friend's face.

"Yeah, man, those dudes are nowhere. I wouldn't worry 'bout them. You can have Black friends. Even in Morton," T.C. told Jeff.

"I don't care about Cap and his pack, T.C.," Jeff tried to assure them. The three boys grew quiet again.

"I've been thinking," Jeff said finally to Lamar, "maybe you and me can do a movie together. We can get students to act in it. We can use my sixteen-millimeter camera. I know we can do it."

"Man, why didn't we think of this before?" Lamar shouted, leaping up from the table. "Let's do it!" He and Jeff slapped five.

"Don't leave me out," T.C. said, looking as if he had eaten too many hamburgers and too much cheesecake.

"You know you're in, T.C.," Lamar said. T.C. mustered enough energy to slap Lamar five the way Lamar had just done with Jeff.

Jeff looked over at Lamar.

"Steven Spielberg started when he was about our age."

"He *did*?" That bit of trivia caught Lamar's attention.

"Yeah. He was twelve when he made his first home movie," Jeff went on.

"What was it about?" Lamar wanted to know.

"A train wreck. He used his own toy trains. Then he made an eight-millimeter film called *The Last Gunfight*. And get this, when he was thirteen, he used his father's movie camera to make a forty-minute war film. His classmates were the actors. And it won first prize in a statewide competition."

"Man, that dude was bad." Lamar beamed, impressed. "That's what we'll be doing."

"I wonder if there's a film contest in Louisiana," Jeff said.

"We can check it out," Lamar replied. "If not, I bet there're other competitions."

"Spike Lee started when he was our age, didn't he, Lamar?"

"No, T.C. Spike said he didn't know he wanted to be a filmmaker until he got to college. He went to Morehouse."

"Oh. So he was like me. He didn't know what he wanted to be when he was young either. I don't feel so bad now."

"I don't know 'bout all that, T.C.," Lamar replied. "But I'm sure not everybody knows what career they wanna do when they're young. Some people figure it out later. So, where we gonna get a script?" Lamar asked, turning to face Jeff. We need a script, don't we?"

"We can write our own script," Jeff answered with confidence. "Each of us can come up with an idea and do a synopsis of it. Then we can choose the one we think is the best. We can work on the final script together."

"That sounds like a plan to me. I'm ready."

T.C. looked confused again. "Hey, guys, I don't wanna sound dumb, but what's a synopsis?"

"T.C., where were you in the Language Arts class when that was covered? A synopsis ain't nothing but a summary, an outline."

"That's all," T.C. responded sheepishly to Lamar's dressing down.

Lamar's mind was racing as he and his two friends left the cafeteria.

We gotta write a synopsis. We've gotta get a location for the shoot. We gotta get actors. We've got a lot of work to do. And I'm going to the council meeting tonight.

CHAPTER 4

The school day had ended. Lamar and T.C. sat on the steps of Lamar's house, waiting for Lamar's grandfather to pick them up for the council meeting. Lamar held his video camcorder.

"Man. He's sure tall, ain't he?" T.C. cracked when they saw Philyaw walking toward them.

"Yeah. I bet you wish you had his skills."

"Yeah. And me and you can't even dribble."

"Speak for yourself, T.C."

Philyaw parked his size-sixteen sneakers on the step next to Lamar.

"What's up, lil' brothers? Kyra home?" he inquired.

"Yeah, she's here," Lamar responded. Then he turned to face the front door. "Kyra! Phil here to see you!"

"Them some bad sneaks, Phil!" T.C. shouted out, his eyes fixed on Philyaw's new basketball shoes.

"LeBron 18," Phil announced proudly. "The latest model. Lakers purple all the way."

"Yeah, man, that purple looks cool. I bet they cost a lot," quipped T.C.

"Yeah, they do. But I don't pay for sneakers anymore. I don't have to. I get all the sneakers I want . . . free."

"You're a bad dude, Phil. You're the man," T.C. said as he kept laying it on.

"Want me to get you dudes a pair? I can get them, you know."

"Yeah! We sure do," T.C. said, jumping up from the steps excitedly.

"What do you want, Phil?"

Kyra sounded curt. Sticking her head out the door, she continued, "I told you I was busy today. I've got things to do."

Phil mumbled, trying to find an answer. But nothing would come. Kyra stood in the doorway, waiting.

"I—I—I told you I wanted you to help me with that test," Phil finally said. "You know I gotta keep my grades up. You said you would help me."

"Where're your books?" Kyra asked, staring Phil down.

"Aw, man! I forgot the books. I was at basketball practice. When it ended, I came right over here."

"Come on in."

Kyra knew she had Phil eating out of her hand.

"I've got my book for that class," she told Phil.

Phil ambled up the steps and walked inside the house. Kyra closed the door behind them.

"Phil got it bad, ain't he?" said T.C., stating the obvious while shaking his head.

"He's in *love,* T.C. He's in love."

"Phil can have almost any girl he wants, even White girls. But he really likes Kyra."

"I tell you, T.C., my sister is awesome. She's gonna finish at the top of her class. And she's getting scholarship offers just like Phil. Kyra's going to be a doctor. Yeah, all the girls flip over Phil, but not Kyra. She knows she's special, too. And Phil knows she's special."

The sound of Lamar's grandfather's old blue Chevy pulling up in front of the house interrupted them.

"Come on, fellas! I don't wanna be late!"

Lamar grabbed his camera, and he and T.C. dashed to Gramps's car. On the way, he remembered he hadn't told his mother he was leaving. So he hurried back to the porch.

"Gramps's here," he yelled to his mother. "We're out."

He and T.C. jumped into the car, Lamar in the front and T.C. in the back. Just before Gramps drove off, Lamar's mom came to the door.

"How ya doing, Papa?" she asked her father-in-law.

"I'm fine, daughter. And how're you?"

"I'm blessed. We miss you at church. When will we see you again?"

"Yeah, I know I've been backsliding. I'll do better," Gramps promised. "I'll try to make it this Sunday."

"I'll be looking for you. And, Lamar, don't forget what your father told you to do when you get back."

"I won't, Mom."

Let's get out of here, Gramps, Lamar thought, *before Mom comes up with a reason for me not to go.*

Finally, his grandfather drove off.

Town Hall sat about twenty yards from the street on Town Hall Court, several blocks from Main Street. The 1980s two-story burgundy brick building had replaced the old town hall from the early 1900s.

Once they arrived, Gramps, Lamar, and T.C. got out of the car and walked quickly inside the building.

"Is this where the meeting gonna be?" T.C. asked just after they entered.

"No. It's on the second floor, T.C.," Gramps answered.

"What's on this floor?" T.C. continued with his questions.

"Different departments," Gramps responded patiently. "Public Works, Town Clerk, Transportation Department.

Permits Department. And others. We gotta take the stairs to the second floor. The elevator ain't working."

When they reached the second floor, Lamar stopped and looked around. To the right and left were offices of the mayor and town council members. Straight ahead were large wooden double doors that led to the council chamber.

"Gramps, you sure it's okay for me to videotape the meeting?" Lamar asked. "I don't wanna get you into trouble."

"You ain't gonna get me in no trouble. I know what I'm doing," he assured his grandson. "I called today, and they said it's okay. They say they like to see young students involved in civic affairs."

As soon as they entered the chamber, Lamar surveyed the room as any good filmmaker would do. About a hundred chairs were arranged in rows in the center of the room. On the dais, nameplates were placed on tables in front of the empty black leather chairs. Two desks, one at each end of the dais, were occupied. Lamar assumed they were for secretaries or clerks.

Lamar noticed that the gray carpeting on the floor looked old and worn, but clean.

Everyone seemed to know Gramps. Lamar began recording their exchanges right away.

"That's my grandson," Gramps told anyone who would listen, pointing to Lamar. "He's gonna be a big director like the brother that directed that *Black Panther* movie."

"Ryan Coogler," Lamar interjected, lowering his video camcorder to provide the name he knew his grandfather had forgotten.

"Yeah! That's his name. Ryan Cooper."

Lamar let the close-but-not-quite-correct attempt go. *Cooper will do for now,* he thought.

Lamar continued to videotape the room, moving from one side to the other. He knew how important it was to establish the location, because it set up the context for important scenes. And the most important scene was the council meeting.

Finally, Gramps took a seat in the front row. Lamar videotaped people as they sat down. Some smiled when the camcorder focused on them. A few turned away, letting Lamar know they didn't want to be videotaped. So he moved on.

Suddenly, a small, smartly dressed group entered the chamber through a rear door behind the dais. All eyes fell upon them as they sat in the chairs that had been assigned to each of them. Lamar didn't know what was going to happen next. So, he stopped videotaping and sat next to Gramps and T.C.

"Did the council people just walk in?" he whispered to his grandfather. Gramps nodded his head yes.

"And the mayor," Gramps added. "The mayor was a councilman before he was elected mayor. The council members represent the five political districts in the town. The meeting will start any minute now."

Lamar looked closely at the six people seated at the dais. He didn't know there were two Black members on the town council. He was aware that the mayor, Herman Johnson, was Black, because his son Michael attended a class with Lamar at Morton Middle School.

"The regular meeting of the Morton Town Council is called to order!" the mayor declared, breaking the momentary silence.

Lamar watched him closely. Dressed in a black suit and white shirt that was unbuttoned at the top, the mayor looked comfortable in his position. Michael had chosen his father as his hero for a class project. So, Lamar knew that, like almost everyone else who held important positions in the town, the mayor was born and raised in Morton.

"Please stand for the Pledge of Allegiance, after which Reverend Nathaniel Carter will lead us in a prayer," the mayor told those who had gathered. The council meeting of the town of Morton was underway. Various reports from council members were presented. The mayor gave an update on the state of the town. Lamar and T.C. weren't interested until Council Member Wilcox shared her report on recreation.

"We're still waiting to receive the grant that will enable us to upgrade our two parks," she told the assembled citizens. "We want to add more playground equipment, such as swing sets and slides. We want to resurface the basketball courts."

That got Lamar's and T.C.'s attention. Sometimes they played on the dilapidated basketball courts at the park on the south side. But the courts were in such bad condition, dribbling a basketball on them was like maneuvering over an obstacle course.

"We have turned in all the required paperwork," Council Member Wilcox continued. "But you know how slow the parish and state move."

"We sho' do need to put some money into the park in our area. It needs a lot of work!" someone yelled out.

"We're aware of that," Council Member Wilcox responded. "We've been working hard on this for some months now."

"Thank you, Council Member Wilcox, for that thorough report," Mayor Johnson said. "I do know how hard you and the committee have been working on getting the funding to upgrade the parks. I want you to know that we appreciate what you're doing."

"Thank you, Mayor." Council Member Wilcox nodded. "It gets frustrating. It's not easy."

"I know it's not. Now. It's that time of the meeting where our citizens have an opportunity to express their concerns and to ask questions," the mayor announced.

As soon as the mayor finished, Gramps leaped to his feet.

"Mr. Phillips, you may speak," the mayor said. "You've become a regular at our meetings again. Good to see you."

The remark drew derisive giggles, especially from several council members. They all knew how determined Gramps could be when he embraced an issue or a cause. He was unrelenting. But Gramps wasn't fazed.

"I know y'all missed me when I wasn't coming here," he told the mayor and the council members. "But I'm back now."

"We're looking forward to what you have to share with us."

"I bet you are, Mayor," Gramps cracked back. "I'm sure I make the council's day when I come here."

"You certainly help to create an exciting meeting. What would you like to share with us?"

"I'm glad y'all look forward to me coming here, Mayor," Gramps replied, gathering himself. "I'm here about an old issue. It's one that we've been told would be addressed but has not been. And that's the paving of the streets in our neighborhoods, the Black neighborhoods. I mean, almost all the White neighborhoods have paved streets. And they have been paved for years. And the town keeps those streets in good condition. But there are so many streets in the Black communities that ain't paved. They really ain't streets. They're roads. Every time it rains, like it did last week, those streets get muddy. And in the summertime when it's dry, dust flies all over the place. Now, y'all said you would find the money to pave those streets. But nothing's been done. So, my question, and this is to all of you up there, is when will our streets be paved?"

By the end of Gramps's monologue, most of the Black citizens were standing and applauding.

"When will our communities receive the same kind of services from the town that White communities get?" Gramps asked, squeezing in one last question.

"Now, Mr. Phillips, you know we've been trying to find the money to get that work done," Mayor Johnson responded, now standing up himself. "There is only so much we can do without the funds we need. We've paved a few streets in the Clarksville section."

Obviously agitated, the mayor tried to appear cool and sat down again. But the look on his face said he wished Gramps would disappear.

Lamar had been watching his grandfather so intently

he had forgotten to start the videotape. He had never seen his Gramps like this before. Lamar picked up his camcorder.

"Yeah, I know. I know, Mayor," Gramps countered. "Three. Mercy, Pine and Walnut. That's it. And you paved them more than a year ago."

Lamar was flowing now, moving from his grandfather to the mayor, from the mayor to his grandfather. Gramps moved closer to the dais, where the mayor was seated. Lamar moved closer, too.

"Tell me this, Mayor Johnson, why are the streets in the White neighborhoods paved? They got streetlights. They even got sidewalks. But we don't have sidewalks. When it comes to our communities, we're always told there ain't enough money!"

Mayor Johnson looked stunned by Gramps's charges. Lamar bet he was probably wondering what the town hall attendees were thinking. Gramps had just accused the council of unequal treatment. Mayor Johnson rose to his feet again, pointing a long finger at Gramps.

"Mr. Phillips, that isn't fair," he blurted out. "You know most of those streets in the White neighborhoods were paved long before I came into office! You know that! You campaigned for me. I'm just trying to do my best for the people as we move forward. I think I've done quite a lot for this town. That's why I was elected."

"All that's good, Mayor. And we appreciate the things you've done," Gramps said, coming back at the mayor. "But we elected you so you could help make life better for all of us. You've put a few Black people in good positions, and that's a good thing. But things ain't changed enough for most of the people, if you know what I mean.

Gramps is right, Lamar thought as he continued to capture all the excitement. *There certainly is action here!*

"Mr. Phillips, I think you're being very unfair," Councilman Burleigh, one of the Black councilmen, jumped in. "It takes time to change things. It can't be done overnight. And you know that as well as anyone!"

"I know things can't change overnight, Councilman Burleigh. But in order for things to change in any meaningful way, y'all got to give some of the problems we Black people face the same kind of priority these White council members give to the problems the folks in their communities face. Move the money from somewhere else and use it to fix the streets. That's what the White council members would do."

Lamar videotaped the three White council members as they watched the interchange, bemused by it all.

The Black people in the room stood and applauded again.

"Tell it like it is!" one of them yelled out.

"Somebody needs to tell them the truth!" sounded off another.

"Thank you, Brother Phillips!" a heavyset lady shouted.

Mayor Johnson looked confused. These were the people who had voted for him in past elections. They were enthusiastic about having one of their own as mayor of a town that for decades had denied them the right to even vote. Raised voices issuing complaints and concerns cascaded throughout the chamber.

Slowly, Mayor Johnson sat back down in his seat and looked out at the animated faces before him. Their outbursts were similar to the way they'd responded to previous White mayors of the town. For several minutes he stayed silent, surveying the room. Finally, he stood up and urged everyone to quiet down. He then turned to Gramps.

"Mr. Phillips, can you come by my office tomorrow?"

"Yes, sir. I sure can," Gramps answered, surprised. "What time?"

"Ten o'clock."

"I'll be there five minutes before ten."

Mayor Johnson took a deep breath. Now he seemed a little more relaxed.

"And if any of you want to join us," he offered in a calmer voice, "you can. I look forward to meeting with you. We have an open-door policy."

When the meeting ended, people rushed to Gramps, patting him on the back and thanking him for speaking up.

"You told them right, Mr. Phillips," a beaming young man said. "We need more people like you. You tell it like it is. You stopped coming to these meetings for a while and believe me, we missed you."

"I'm back now. I'm back," Gramps assured him.

"Thank God for you, Mr. Phillips," an older lady added with tears in her eyes.

Lamar kept taping. He couldn't be prouder of Gramps.

CHAPTER 5

On the way home, Gramps was quiet. Lamar had expected him to continue talking about all the things that were wrong in Morton. But his grandfather had toned down.

Maybe he's waiting for me and T.C. to say something, he thought.

"Gramps, I'm glad we went to the meeting," he told his grandfather. "I learned a lot."

"Me too," T.C. seconded.

"You really spoke up, Gramps," Lamar continued. "I didn't know you could speak like that. You're another Reverend Al."

"Lamar, I ain't no Reverend Al," Gramps corrected him. "I'm just doing what needs to be done. I feel sorry for the mayor and the Black council members. They got tough jobs. The White people with money moved away when Black folks got a little power. And they took their money with them. So there's not enough money in the town's budget to do all the things that need to be done. But if we don't speak up, that little money will still go to help White people, not us. The mayor gotta know that he's got to make *us* the priority sometimes. There has been some progress, but this town is still segregated. So when the White communities are given the priority, we get left out. It ain't enough to put a few Black people in offices while the rest of us are suffering.

"I like the mayor. He's a good man. You just gotta push him to be more courageous about the things the whole town needs, not just some parts of the town."

"Why don't you run for mayor, Gramps?" Lamar suggested, his face animated by his brilliant idea. "Me and T.C. can help you with your campaign. And I can shoot commercials for you."

"No, that ain't me," Gramps replied. "I'm not cut out to be no politician. I'm an agitator, like W. E. B. Du Bois and Ida B. Wells were. You know Ida used her pen and her voice. W. E. B. was a thinker and a man of words. Of course, y'all know Malcolm and Dr. King. I'm not comparing myself to those Black giants, but I got a little of their spirit and fight."

Lamar and T.C. nodded and said "YEAH!" But

Gramps didn't pay them much attention. He had something else on his mind.

"I got to get you boys some good books to read. You need to have *more* relevant material to read other than those few books you have at school. There's so much Black history you need to know. You know what they say, knowledge is power. I'll give you some of my books and you can read them, and we'll discuss what you read. How does that sound?"

"I wanna start reading more anyway," Lamar said. "In order to be a good filmmaker, you have to know a lot of stuff, right, Gramps?"

"Yeah, that's true, Lamar. But you need to know a lotta stuff, period. I'd love for y'all to come by my house for a visit."

"That'll be cool."

"Like Lamar said, that'll be cool," added T.C.

As his car moved slowly away from downtown Morton, Gramps was quiet once more. Lamar wondered what he was thinking. He looked back at T.C. His friend was fighting to stay awake. Lamar smiled at him. *Just like T.C.,* he thought.

"You know, since Grandma Ella died, I've been in that ol' house all by myself. It'll be good to have some company."

Lamar was surprised by how sad Gramps now sounded.

"It'll be good to visit you again, Gramps."

Lamar knew how close his grandfather and Grandma Ella had been. They were always together. If his Ella were still living, she would have been at the council meeting tonight, standing right beside Gramps. And speaking up, too. Grandma Ella was just as tough and as smart as her husband.

Lamar remembered when he was much younger, his family visited his grandparents' house often. There were family dinners at Thanksgiving, Christmas and the Fourth of July. Grandma Ella cooked different kinds of delicious dishes. Sometimes, the kids would eat and then play until late at night. Uncle Robert, Lamar's father's brother, and his family would drive down from Thomasville. His father's youngest brother, they called him Rich, had moved to Dallas years ago. But sometimes he would drive across the country to join the family gathering. Eloise, their sister, and her daughter always came, too.

But after Grandma Ella died, that all stopped. Gramps wanted to be by himself. He rarely left the house. After more than fifty years together, he just found it difficult to go on without his partner, without his other half. That was more than a year ago. Lamar hadn't visited him very often during that period. His friends and classmates had taken up most of his time. And there was his interest in being a filmmaker. Connecting with his grandfather now reminded him how much he had missed.

As Gramps drove through the south side, Lamar knew that Grandma Ella was on his grandfather's mind. When they reached T.C.'s house, T.C. didn't want to get out of the car.

"Ah, man, this is a downer," he protested. "I like being around you, Mr. Phillips."

"We'll get together again," Gramps assured him.

T.C. jumped from the car and dashed into his house, smiling from ear to ear.

"You got the excitement you were looking for?" Gramps asked Lamar as he parked in front of Lamar's house.

"I sure did, Gramps," Lamar responded enthusiastically. "I sure did."

"You got some good footage?"

"Yes, sir. As soon as I get home, I'm gonna check it out. I got a lot of good stuff. I got you giving it to them council people. I'm glad you told us about the meeting. We've been racking our brains trying to find something important to videotape in this ol' country town."

"Well, you know, there used to be a whole lot more going on here."

"For real?" Lamar asked.

A whole lot going on in Morton, he thought. *That sounds funny.*

Gramps relaxed as he settled in his seat and stared out the front window. The front lights of his car illuminated the dark street.

"When I was round your age," he shared, "there was twice as many people round here than there is now. On Saturdays, the town would be full of people coming to the stores to buy stuff after a long week of working. Most of those stores are closed now. And most of the newer businesses went to the two shopping malls that were built outside of town."

"But, Gramps, there ain't nothing in those shopping malls either but places like Popeyes, McDonald's and a few banks. There ain't no museums. No bookstores. Only one movie theater. Ain't nothing here."

"That's why people like your daddy had to go to Thomasville to find work. You see, Lamar, most people around here used to work on farms. This was a farming area. People grew cotton, corn, hay and crops like that. That's all changed now."

"Yeah, but that was a bad time for Black people, wasn't it, Gramps?"

"You got that right. Most of us struggled to make ends meet. You think it's segregated now? Back then it was way worse. We couldn't vote. We couldn't stay in that raggedy motel in town. We couldn't even drink water from the same water fountains that White people drank from. So some of us decided to do something about it. That was in 1966. We started protesting, demonstrating and boycotting White businesses. It was mostly young people. I was in high school then. So was your Grandma Ella. Yes, sir, that's when the Civil Rights Movement came to Morton. Me and your grandma were some kind of freedom fighters. That's what they called us."

"Did you get beat up?" Lamar asked curiously.

"I sure did. I went to jail, too. Grandma Ella, too. It got so rough in Morton, reporters from the national news networks came to cover what was going on. And for the first time, people in other places were talking about this little ol' town."

"So what happened, Gramps?"

"We changed some things. It took time, but some of the White businesses in town started hiring Black people, including the bank where your mother work at now. The Colored Only signs went down. The White-only schools were integrated."

"Yeah, but they're mostly Black now," Lamar jumped in. "Ain't but a few White students at Morton Middle School. At the high school, too."

"That's because some White parents took their kids out of the public schools and built private ones," Gramps responded. "They didn't want their children going to school with no Black kids."

Lamar clutched his video camcorder, closed his eyes and breathed deeply. "If I was born then, I would have been right there, filming everything. I would have been protesting, too." Gramps smiled.

"Well, you better go inside," Gramps suggested. "I've been parked here for a good while now."

"I'm sure glad you spoke up at that council meeting."

"Somebody has to, Lamar. We've made some progress. But there're a lot of folks who want to take us back. We can't sit still and let that happen."

"I don't think it's that bad, do you, Gramps? I mean, we got it a lot better than you had when you was younger."

"Lamar, it is somewhat better. If we don't admit that we've made some progress, we would be dishonoring those who fought for that progress. But we got a long way to go before Black folks are treated fairly and receive equal justice. You see, every generation pass the baton on to the next to carry on the struggle. And look what's happening now. Folks are trying to undo the progress that has been made."

Gramps's observation didn't register much with Lamar. He turned to his grandfather with a different thought on his mind.

"Gramps, I remember seeing you in that postal

worker's uniform when I was a little boy. You used to deliver mail at the preschool I went to. Remember? I used to tell all the kids, that's my grandfather! How long did you work for the post office?"

"I worked there for twenty-five years, Lamar," Gramps answered. "I was the second Black person hired to work in the post office in Morton. Calvin Henderson was hired two weeks before me. We did better on the civil service tests than anybody, even the Whites. Man, those folks put up a fight to stop us from getting those jobs. Both Calvin and me were Vietnam veterans. That made it more difficult for them to keep us from being hired. Calvin is dead now. Yes, sir, I was at that post office for twenty-five years."

Gramps leaned toward his grandson and placed his large hand on his shoulder.

"Listen, son, now is your time. It's your generation that's got the future in its hands. You have to seize the time. You understand what I mean?"

"Yes, sir. You have to take advantage of the opportunities you get."

"That's it!" Gramps responded enthusiastically. "And sometimes you have to make your opportunities," he added. "I wanna spend more time with you, Lamar," Gramps said. "I know your daddy and mama are busy and all. It took me a while, you know, to get my bearings back after your grandmother made her transition. But I'm good now. I know she's right here with me. Yes, sir! I feel like my old self again. It's nothing like doing something that really makes a difference in people's lives. Something that brings about change, makes life better for your people. You never get too old for that."

Lamar looked at Gramps in a way that he had never done before. His grandfather was always, well, just his Gramps. He had never heard much about his grandparents' civil rights contributions. As he studied the lines, the wrinkles and the rough aging, the man next to him was more than just Gramps, someone Lamar had taken for granted. It was interesting to hear about what his grandfather did during the civil rights days. But that was so long ago.

"You wouldn't mind hanging out with an oldster like me, would you?" Gramps asked Lamar.

"I'd love it, Gramps."

Gramps turned to get a better look at his grandson.

"What're you doing on Saturday afternoon?"

"Saturday afternoon?"

Lamar moved his camera from his right to his left hand, thinking about Gramps's question.

"Nothing, I guess," he finally answered. "Probably just hanging out with T.C. after I finish my chores at home."

"Come by the house around two o'clock. I got a good

documentary I want you to see. And bring T.C. with you. Bring some friends. They need to see it, too."

"That's a bet, Gramps. I'll see you on Saturday."

Gramps waited until his grandson had walked into the house. Then he drove off, smiling broadly.

CHAPTER 6

"How's the synopsis going?" Jeff asked.

"What?" Lamar held his cell phone closer to his ear so he could hear better.

"I said, how's the synopsis going?" Jeff repeated.

"I'm working on it. I worked on it this morning after I finished my chores. Too bad we can't hook up at your house or mine so we can work on it together. My folks wouldn't mind you coming over here."

"My parents would," Jeff responded, sounding agitated. "Anyway, I've got a lot done. But I have to leave in a little while. My dad wants me to go with him to the golf course. I don't like golf. I don't think he likes it either. He just wanna hang out with friends. It's another Saturday going to waste for me."

"I'm going to hang out with my grandfather. He's real cool, man."

"All right. But don't forget about our synopsis."

"Yep. You got it. Check you later."

As soon as Lamar got off the phone, he heard T.C.

"Let's go, Junior. We're waiting for you."

"That knucklehead," Lamar mumbled to himself. "I've told him not to call me that."

Lamar grabbed his video camcorder and hurried out the door, where T.C. and two friends waited for him in the yard. As soon as he reached T.C., he hit him with a gentle punch.

"What you do that for?"

"I've told you 'bout that Junior."

"Man, that hurt!" T.C. complained, massaging the aching spot.

"You know that didn't hurt, T.C.," Lamar said.

"You gonna take that?" one of the friends asked T.C.

"We just funning, Ray," T.C. said. "It ain't nothing."

Lamar and T.C. had known Ray since first grade. He lived in the same neighborhood. But lately Lamar and T.C. had noticed a change. Ray didn't seem to enjoy the things the three friends used to do together, and he had begun hanging out with Frankie Pierce and Jimmy Clay.

"It ain't no big deal, Ray. We're all friends," the fourth member of the group said.

Little John had moved to Morton when they were in the fourth grade. His family called him Little John, and so everyone else did, too. But he wasn't really little. In fact, he was heavier than his three friends.

"Nobody asked you anything," Ray shot back.

As the quartet walked down Clay Street, the road that Lamar's grandfather lived on, Lamar remembered how Gramps had talked about the unpaved roads. He hadn't really given them much thought before. Like everyone else, he was just used to the streets being the way they were.

As Lamar and his friends got closer to Lamar's grandfather's house, he thought about the old oak tree in the yard that he used to climb. Sometimes he would lay on his back underneath the big branches and look up through the leaves at the clouds above as they floated past. He remembered the old car tire Gramps hung on one of the tree's large branches that became a swing for the children. Gramps's house was one of the oldest ones on Clay Street. He and Grandma Ella had built it just after they were married. It was where Lamar's father, his father's two brothers and his sister were born and raised.

When the four boys reached the yard, Lamar saw that the old tire was still there, and a warm feeling filled him.

They mounted the steps of the white-framed house. After Lamar knocked on the door, Gramps opened it right away.

"Come on in, fellas," he invited them.

Lamar was drawn to the photograph on the wall across the room. It was Gramps and Grandma Ella on their wedding day. He had seen it before but rarely paid attention to it. This time, he stared at the photograph, amazed at how young Gramps and Grandma Ella looked. Gramps had a long Afro and a short goatee like some Black men wore back in the day. Grandma Ella wore an Afro, too. As Lamar looked closer, he thought Grandma Ella looked like Kyra, or rather, Kyra looked like Grandma Ella. She had the same tan skin color as her grandmother. Their eyes were similar, too: brown, bright and radiant.

"I got everything all set up," Gramps told his young visitors. "I got snacks, too."

"What kind of snacks?" Lamar asked, ready to dive in.

"They're on that table over there," Gramps answered, pointing to a big tray of finger food.

The four boys rushed over, expecting delicious treats like popcorn and potato chips they could chow down on. But what they saw was not what they expected.

"I don't see any snacks," Ray blurted out dejectedly. "There ain't nothing here but carrots, broccoli, celery and junk like that."

"That's healthy food," Gramps replied as he walked over, grabbed a carrot stick and bit down on it. "It's good for you."

"I love carrots," Little John declared, snatching a carrot stick from the tray and holding it up in his hand. "I love broccoli, too. My mom fix this kind of stuff all the time."

"You're a pig," Ray belted out to Little John. "Man, this ain't cool. Mr. Phillips, you a vegan?"

"Well, not quite. But I watch what I eat. Most of the processed foods we eat ain't good for us. You boys should watch what you put into your bodies, too."

"You mean, we ain't gonna have popcorn, potato chips and soda while we watch this movie?" Ray complained.

"Come on, Ray," Lamar told him. "We don't have to have all that to watch the documentary."

"Speak for yourself," Ray shot back.

Gramps ignored all the fuss. He was focused on the movie he had planned to show.

"Y'all sit down so I can start the documentary," he directed. "You guys are gonna learn some important stuff today."

Ray shook his head, still agitated that the food he wanted wasn't being served. He grabbed a seat in front of the large-screen television along with the others.

"Do any of you know much about Ida B. Wells-

Barnett?" Gramps asked. "Not just her name. But who she really was?"

"Yeah, I know she was a civil rights leader back in the day," Lamar answered proudly.

"Well, that's partly right," Gramps said. "But not the civil rights period of the 1950s and 1960s. Ida. B. Wells came decades before that. She started her work for freedom in the late 1800s. She led a campaign against the lynching of Black folks in the 1890s and helped to establish the NAACP. She was awesome."

"Is this what we came here for?" Ray asked pointedly, rising from his seat. "I thought we were gonna see a real movie, like the ones they show in the theater at the mall. I don't wanna see nothing 'bout no civil rights."

"Come on, Ray," T.C. admonished. "You'll enjoy it. Sit down."

"I ain't gonna enjoy nothing." Ray hurried toward the door. "Y'all fooled me over here."

"Before you go, Ray," Gramps said, rushing to intercept him, "can you tell me why you don't wanna know more about your people, about those who helped to make things better for you?"

"All that stuff don't mean nothing to me, Mr. Phillips," Ray answered rudely. "What good's it gonna do me to know what people did before I was even born?"

"If you stay here, I'll tell you why," Gramps answered,

looking Ray directly in the eye, hoping he could find a way to convince him not to leave.

"Naw. I got better things to do with my time," Ray spouted off. "I mean, I appreciate you, Mr. Phillips. But this ain't me. I don't care about all that Black stuff."

"It makes me sad to hear you say that, Ray. It makes me real sad."

Gramps turned away, but then, not giving up, he faced Ray again.

"Don't you watch the news? Don't you see what's happening in the country? We got a lot of work to do to make things right. People like me, the old heads? We'll be gone. But it's your generation that's got to continue the fight."

"I don't mean to hurt your feelings, Mr. Phillips," Ray said in a firm voice. "You being an elder and all. But I don't see what all that stuff got to do with me. You know what I mean? I appreciate you, though. But I'm trying to get ahead. That stuff ain't gonna help me do that."

"Let him go, Gramps," Lamar told his grandfather. "We shouldn't have asked him to come in the first place."

"Y'all should've told me what this was about," Ray yelled. "It would of saved my time and yours, too. Check y'all later."

Ray dashed out the door, leaving it slightly open. Gramps watched him bound down the steps. After Ray left the yard, Gramps closed the door gently and returned to the room.

"I shouldn't have brought Ray here, Gramps," Lamar apologized after seeing the look of dejection on his grandfather's face. He knew how excited Gramps had been about sharing the movie with him and his friends.

"Don't worry about it, Lamar," Gramps answered. "You can't win over everybody."

Lamar knew that Ray's attitude had upset his grandfather. But as soon as the documentary started, Gramps perked up. He was his old self again.

CHAPTER 7

"Lamar! Gramps is blowing for you," Lamar's mom yelled from the kitchen.

Lamar rushed outside, where his grandfather's old blue Chevrolet was parked. His grandfather wore that big smile, so Lamar knew he had something up his sleeve.

"Hi, Gramps. What's up?"

"What ya doing?"

"Working on something for school. But I'm finished now."

"You wanna go for a ride?"

"A ride?" Lamar asked quizzically.

"Yeah. It won't take long."

"I guess so."

Lamar rushed to his room and picked up his video camcorder.

"I'm going with Gramps," he told his mother as he ran past her to his grandfather's car. Lamar's mom nodded her approval.

Lamar had no idea where his grandfather was going. He was curious but didn't want to ask. *Maybe Gramps wanna surprise me,* he thought.

After driving through town, they reached a long, narrow, two-lane highway, miles away. There were no commercial buildings. No houses. For the first few miles, there were only tall green pine trees that stretched as far as Lamar could see. He eyed them closely. *Look like they're reaching for the sky,* he thought.

As they continued down the highway, the scene changed quickly. Stalks of corn, their green leaves waving in the air, dominated the fertile land on both sides of the highway. Gramps didn't say a word. He continued to drive slowly, looking straight ahead. That all changed when small green scrubs replaced the corn.

"That's cotton," Gramps told Lamar. "By July or August, you'll see white cotton bolls all over the place. When I was your age, I picked cotton in fields like that. Me and my whole family and almost everybody else I knew. Now they got machines to do that work."

"I don't think I could've done that, Gramps," Lamar told his grandfather defiantly. "No cotton picking for me."

"All young people say what they wouldn't have done

if they lived in those days," Gramps declared. "It's easy to say that after so many people done fought and died to change things," he added in a gentler voice.

"I don't know, Gramps. Young Black people today are brave. Look at the Bloods and Crips. I don't wanna be a member. But they don't take nothing from nobody."

"You don't think Black people were brave during those times?" Gramps asked, raising his voice. "You say young Black people are brave now," he continued without waiting for a response. "You know what? Black people were brave then, too. They had to be. If they weren't, *you* wouldn't be here. You can be brave today, as you say, because Black people *were strong* back in the day, too.

"Do you think you just became brave all of a sudden? Lamar, you young people are standing on the shoulders of some real brave and strong people. They gave their lives to make life better for you and other young people like you."

Gramps went quiet again, focusing on the road before him.

As Lamar looked out the window, he thought about the conversation he and his grandfather had just had. He had never really thought about Black people being strong during slavery or during the civil rights days. Maybe a few, like Sojourner Truth, Harriet Tubman, Frederick Douglass and Dr. Martin Luther King, the ones everyone talked about during Black History Month. Now he knew more about Ida B. Wells-Barnett from Gramps's documentary. But Lamar thought, if Black people were strong, why were they enslaved so long and treated as second-class citizens for so many years?

"Gramps, what do you mean Black people were strong back then? I mean back in the day?"

"Lamar, you don't think Black people fought back during slavery and Jim Crow? There were thousands of revolts all over the country during slavery led by enslaved Black people. Thousands and thousands were killed fighting back. Black people have been fighting for their freedom ever since we been in this country, even when the challenges were almost insurmountable.

"It's our fault," he said softly to his grandson, a look of guilt now visible on his face. "Me, your dad, your mom, the school. None of us have done a good enough job sharing the real history of Black people. We dropped the ball. Knowing your history, who you *really* are, helps prepare you for most anything.

"So much has happened that you don't know. Why, you weren't even born when Barack Obama was elected the first Black president. You didn't experience the excitement and joy of that historic event. And you were only two years old when he was elected for the second time. Time sho' does pass so quickly."

Lamar rolled down the window and felt the wind blow

against his face. His grandfather's eyes were fixed on the road ahead. Gramps pulled over to the side, got out of the car and looked around as if searching for something.

"That road gotta be somewhere around here," he said to himself.

After getting back into the car, he drove another hundred feet or so and stopped once more.

"This looks like it," he mumbled as he got out of the car.

He stood before an old dirt road that was bordered by rows of trees. The road was filled with holes, and grass covered much of it. Gramps got back into the car and drove slowly down the old road. Tree branches struck the car as it passed them. Lamar rolled up the window so they wouldn't hit him.

After a while, the road ended, and before them was an open area covered with green grass, assorted bushes and other vegetation. Gramps stared at it for a while, then got out of the car and walked over. Lamar didn't know whether he should join him.

Is this something special? he thought. *Would Gramps appreciate being disturbed?*

"Lamar, come here. I wanna show you something," Gramps called.

Lamar grabbed his video camcorder and ran to where his grandfather stood.

"You see this stretch of land right there?" Gramps asked him, pointing to an area a few yards away. "The house I grew up in was right in the middle of that. Yep. Sure was. It's gone now. But that's where it was."

Gramps stood motionless, his eyes glued to the area he had pointed out to Lamar. Although only a few moments passed, it seemed more like an hour to Lamar. He wondered again what his grandfather was thinking. But he didn't say anything.

"It wasn't much, but it was home," Gramps said again. "My mama and daddy raised four boys and two girls in that house."

Lamar followed him as he walked farther toward the plot that once held his family home, kicking grass away with his feet as he went.

"That house was right about here." He stopped and pointed with his finger.

Lamar began videotaping, alternating between his grandfather and the patch of land that had captured his grandfather's attention.

"We had a well about thirty yards over there where we got our water," Gramps continued. "Didn't have no plumbing then. And an outdoor toilet was way over there. Sometimes, when it got cold, we didn't want to go outside. And see where those big bushes are? That's the area where we used to play. We had good times. We sure did."

Lamar listened and videotaped. Videotaped and listened.

"A White man named Claude Turner owned this land. And the house, too. In fact, he owned much of the land in this area. Mama and Daddy paid him to rent the house. Of course, we had to work the crops Old Man Claude grew, like cotton and sugarcane. He let us grow crops on the land in back of the house. Things like collard greens, corn, cabbage, beans, peas and watermelon. Daddy and Mama would scrape up enough money to buy other things we needed, sugar, flour and such. We raised pigs and chickens, too. We never had much money. But we got by."

Lamar followed as his grandfather walked farther ahead. It seemed to Lamar that his Gramps wasn't with him now. He was in another time, another place.

"As soon as the sun came up in the morning," Gramps went on, his eyes transfixed on the ground in front of him, "we had to be out in that cotton field, either hoeing the grass away when it was growing or picking the cotton when it was ready. We didn't stop working until it was too dark to see. As soon as we were old enough, 'bout six or seven, we were in those fields. Some of those cotton fields were so big, you couldn't see the end. It was like standing on a beach looking for the end of the ocean."

Lamar was now full of questions. The world Gramps described was foreign to him.

"You didn't go to school, Gramps?" Lamar asked.

"School?" Gramps let out a haunting laugh and threw up his hands at the thought. "No. Very seldom did we go to school. School wasn't as important as working in those fields. Anyway, we had to walk for miles to get there when we *could* go. I was twelve when I was able to go to school on a regular basis. That was after we moved, when Daddy and Mama found a small house in Morton."

"So, you lived here for twelve years?"

Gramps let in a deep breath of air and released it.

"Yes, twelve long years. But they weren't all bad. We had fun. We loved each other. Daddy and Mama did all they could for us. We were a happy family."

"What happened to the house?"

"Lamar, you're talking 'bout a long time ago. That ole house probably rotted away. I'm surprised this area hasn't been overtaken by trees like everything else round here."

As Gramps walked slowly back to the car, Lamar stopped videotaping and followed, watching his grandfather closely. The shoulders of his grandfather's long, lean, six-feet, two-inch frame had begun to droop. Lamar paid close attention to his long arms and big hands.

Could Gramps have been a great baseball player when he

was much younger? Lamar thought. *Or maybe an all-star football player like Dad?* One thing was sure, Gramps was a *good* man.

"I'm glad you took me to see the place where you were born and where you grew up," Lamar told Gramps on the way home. "I'm learning a lot."

"I'm glad, too," Gramps answered. "I should have brought you here long before now. You come from strong people, Lamar. You gotta know that. You got that good, tough stuff inside you, too. And you gotta know and you gotta believe that. And stop hanging round kids like that Ray."

"You know what I wanna do, Gramps? I wanna do a documentary on you," Lamar blurted out. "I didn't know all this about you."

"A documentary?" Gramps asked quizzically.

Lamar held his breath, wondering what his grandfather was going to say about having a documentary done about his life.

"What for? What kind of documentary? My life ain't worth no documentary."

"Yes it is, Gramps. All that stuff you been telling me about. The civil rights days and all that. It'll make a good documentary."

"You think so?"

"I know so, Gramps."

"Umm. That might be interesting. You're gonna use your camcorder?"

"Yes. It won't be a documentary like the one about Ida B. Wells. But it'll be a good one," Lamar said confidently.

"You're something, Lamar," he told his grandson. "I'll start getting myself together to make it easy for you. Yeah! That's a good thing. My grandson thinking enough of his old granddad to do a documentary on him. You can't beat that. See, that's what I mean by seizing the time!"

Lamar had never given his grandfather a fist bump before. But this time he did.

CHAPTER 8

"How's it going?" Jeff wanted to know. Lamar sat at a table in the school's media center next to his friend.

"I think it's okay. What about you?" he asked Jeff.

"I changed what I was gonna write about," Jeff told Lamar.

"Why? What're you writing 'bout now?"

"I'm still working it out. But I want to write about something that is really meaningful. So I decided to do an outline about alcoholism."

"Alcoholism?" That really caught Lamar's attention.

"Yeah!" Jeff answered, leaning closer. "Did you see *Days of Wine and Roses,* starring Jack Lemmon?"

Jeff didn't wait for Lamar's answer.

"It's about a character named Joe Clay and his wife, Kirsten, who become alcoholics, and their lives tumble out of control because of it. It's a great movie. Lee Remick plays Kirsten, and Jack Lemmon is Joe Clay."

"That's a heavy subject, Jeff. But it sounds interesting."

"You gotta have something that offers real content, you know," Jeff informed Lamar.

Lamar wondered why Jeff had chosen alcoholism as a theme. *Is someone in his family an alcoholic?* he thought. Lamar was curious, but he didn't want Jeff to feel bad.

"In my outline," Jeff continued, "the alcoholics will be a middle school student and his girlfriend. I got a good start on it."

"An alcoholic in middle school?" Lamar asked Jeff. "You don't mean they're *real* alcoholics, do you?"

"No. Not like adults. But if they keep drinking, they could be," Jeff answered.

"Um . . . cool," Lamar said, somewhat relieved. He couldn't imagine someone his age being an alcoholic like those he saw on the streets sometimes.

"So you think it's a good idea?"

"Yeah, it sounds like it, Jeff. I wanna see how you write it."

Jeff beamed at Lamar.

"I'm going to do a documentary on my grandfather," Lamar offered, now anxious to share his good news. "He was a civil rights leader when he was in high school. I'm gonna tell his story and my grandmother's, too. They worked together."

Lamar waited for Jeff's reaction. But Jeff didn't respond at all. He stared at the notepad that he had placed on the table in front of him.

"My grandfather was one of the leaders of the civil rights movement right here in Morton," Lamar went on. "He got arrested and everything. I wanna get the whole story in a documentary."

"But, Lamar, I thought we were gonna do a movie together?" Jeff interjected. "What about *our* project?"

"We're still gonna do it. Ain't nothing changed. I'm still writing an outline for our project. When we both finish, we'll decide which one is the best, right? This is something else I'll be working on."

"So, what's the purpose of the documentary?" he asked, glancing side-eyed at Lamar, obviously agitated.

"What's the purpose? Jeff, I'd be capturing history. History that took place right here in Morton. It's my grandparents' story."

Jeff looked away and Lamar wondered what was wrong.

"What's up?" Lamar asked as Jeff rose from his seat and headed for the exit.

"Nothing," Jeff answered in an unconvincing voice. "I'll be glad when I graduate so I can leave this town. Morton is the pits." With that, Jeff exited.

Lamar sat at the table, wondering what had just happened. Then it came to him. Civil rights and Morton. *They don't go together with a lot of folks around here,* he thought. *Too many people still holding on to the old ways. That's why I can't visit Jeff and why Jeff ain't allowed to visit me. We can only share our friendship at school. Maybe that's why Jeff said he'd be glad to move away.*

"Lamar, Principal Deloria wants to see you in his office," a student who had just entered the media center told Lamar, startling him. "He said to bring your book bag," he added, leaving as abruptly as he had entered.

"Take my book bag?" Lamar asked. "What for?"

Ms. Hamilton, Mr. Deloria's secretary, had just completed a telephone call when Lamar entered.

"Go right in to see Mr. Deloria," she told Lamar. "He's waiting for you."

Principal Deloria was seated at his desk, a stack of papers in front of him. He rose when he saw Lamar. His office was a foreign place to Lamar. Unlike some of the other students, he had never had to go to the principal's office to be counseled or disciplined. He looked around to see what it was like. He wished he had his camcorder.

"Hi, Lamar," Mr. Deloria said. "Your parents want you to come home."

"Come home?" Lamar asked.

"Yes, your father called just a few minutes ago. He'll explain why when you get there."

Lamar's mind started racing. *What's up? What's going on?* He put on his backpack and turned to leave.

"Lamar . . . ," Principal Deloria called to him. Lamar turned around.

"You take care, all right?"

Looking confused, Lamar said, "Yes, sir," and left.

On the way, he wondered why his parents wanted him to come home. Students weren't allowed to use cell phones during the school day. So, as usual, his cell phone had been turned off. But he decided to check to see if anyone had tried to call. He saw his dad's cell number, but there was no message.

Dad probably remembered I couldn't use my phone at school, he thought. *That's why he called the school office.*

What's up? What's going on? Did Kyra have to come home, too? The questions kept on coming.

As he approached the house, Lamar saw a police car

parked in front. Now his mind really started to race. He ran the remainder of the way and rushed inside. His father stood talking to two police officers. Kyra sat on the sofa; her arms were wrapped around their mother, who was sobbing. It all seemed surreal, so different from what it had been like before he had left for school.

Everything had been normal. His mother and father had gotten their usual early start for work. Lamar had even put up with another of Kyra's dress downs when he forgot to remove his plate and glass from the dining room table following breakfast. Now no one noticed him as he stood in the doorway.

"Something's wrong here, Sergeant Ford," Lamar's father told one of the officers, obviously rattled. "Something's wrong."

"I guarantee you we'll look into it, Mr. Phillips," Sergeant Ford said, trying to reassure Lamar's father. "I give you my word on that."

"Where is he now?" Lamar's dad inquired in a subdued voice.

"He's at the hospital. That's where he was taken, and that's where he expired."

Expired? That word hit Lamar like a bolt of lightning. His knees buckled and his heart beat rapidly. He knew what *expired* meant. He had heard that word on the television news. Sometimes, the teachers at school used it. He knew it meant someone had died. But who? His mother and father were there. So was Kyra. Was it Uncle Robert? Aunt Eloise? Everyone knew what had happened but him. He rushed over to his father.

"Dad! Dad!" he called out, frantically pulling his father's arm. "What's going on? What happened? Who died?"

Lamar's dad placed a large hand on his son's shoulder and looked him directly in his eyes.

"Gramps is dead, Lamar. Somebody shot and killed him this morning."

"What? Gramps is dead?!" Lamar asked to make sure he had heard correctly.

"Yes, son, he is," his father said in a definitive voice.

Gramps is dead! This must be a dream, Lamar thought. *Gramps can't be dead! This must be a dream. It will soon end and everything will be normal again. The police officers won't be here. Mom and Dad will be at work. Kyra will be at school practicing for a debate or attending a meeting. Soon, this frightening, nightmarish dream will be over. Everything will go back to the way it's supposed to be.*

But seeing Kyra comforting their mother reminded him that it wasn't a dream. Seeing the police officers talking to his father did, too.

It must be true! His beloved Gramps must be dead!

As the tears rolled down his face, Lamar wanted to ask questions, to say something, to say anything. But the words just wouldn't come. He felt like he wanted to scream. He couldn't do that either. Crying was all he could do at the moment. So he cried. Long and hard. The tears streamed down like a water faucet turned fully open. His father grabbed him and held him close. Kyra and his mother held on to each other. The Phillips family tried desperately, fiercely, to cope with the heart-wrenching tragedy that had been thrust upon them. Pain, anguish and a profound sense of loss filled the room. The two officers stood statue-still, not knowing what to do or say.

"Another Black person killed by White violence against Black people!" Kyra yelled out, breaking the long moment of silence and closeness. "If it ain't the police, it's a crazy White person! Why did that man shoot my grandfather?"

The two officers, extremely uncomfortable, looked away.

"I ask again, why he killed my grandfather?" Kyra demanded.

"Well, that's something that's gotta be looked into," Sergeant Ford answered.

"Something *is* wrong," Kyra told her father. She left

her mother and walked to where her father stood, still embracing Lamar.

"The man who shot Gramps can't get away with this, Dad!" she cried. "He can't!"

"There will be a thorough investigation," Sergeant Ford spoke up, trying to assure the family again. But no one wanted to hear that now. The sergeant continued anyway. "We will find out the truth."

"Yeah! Right!" Kyra snapped at him, and walked back to the sofa to comfort her mother again.

"Is the man who shot my father under arrest?" Lamar's dad inquired, looking directly at the sergeant.

"He's being questioned now," Sergeant Ford answered.

"Questioned? He should be in jail for shooting my grandfather," Kyra shouted, leaping up again. "He should be in jail!"

"We can drive you to the hospital to view the body if you'd like," Sergeant Ford offered, ignoring Kyra's declaration.

"Yeah! Yeah!" Lamar's dad answered quickly, moving around the room aimlessly, as if he didn't know what to do. "Yeah. I wanna see him," he told Sergeant Ford again, nodding his head up and down. He walked slowly toward the door.

"I'm going with you, Daddy!" Kyra hurried to catch up.

"I wanna go, too!" Lamar called out. "I wanna go!"

"No, son. You stay here with your mother. We don't wanna leave her alone."

Lamar's dad gave him another long embrace, then planted a gentle kiss on his wife's cheek, and he, Kyra and the two police officers left.

Lamar walked to the sofa and sat down next to his mother.

"What happened, Mom?" he asked her painfully. "Who shot Gramps?"

Lamar's mom sat upright and stared across the room.

"They say he and a White man got into an argument. The White man said your grandfather threatened him with a gun. So he shot him in self-defense."

"*What?!* Gramps didn't own a gun," Lamar responded automatically. "I ain't never seen him with a gun. He wouldn't harm nobody. Not Gramps."

"I know. I know," Lamar's mother answered solemnly. She rose from the sofa and walked to the window and peered out toward the street.

"Where did this happen, Mom?" Lamar asked, following her.

"Near Highway 76," she answered. "Papa must have been on his way to Thomasville."

Lamar's mother reached for her son and held him in a firm embrace. They both cried as they clung to each other.

"I loved that man." She cried out for her father-in-law in a loud, pained voice. "I *loved* that man. He would do anything for anybody. He was a good man."

"I was just getting to know him," Lamar added, disheartened by the thought of his grandfather not being around anymore. "I was *just* getting to really know him."

CHAPTER 9

Everyone in Morton now knew about the death of Joshua Phillips. That evening, the Phillipses' house was packed with people who had come to offer condolences. Members of their church had come. Neighbors and co-workers were there.

Piled high on the Phillipses' dining room table and kitchen counter were platters of fried chicken, potato salad, cooked vegetables, salads and drinks that church members had brought.

The house was full of chatter. Most folks talked about the kind and thoughtful man Joshua Phillips had been. Some shared stories about their experiences with him. Others told how Joshua Phillips had helped them out of one crisis or another. They all agreed their friend shouldn't have been killed the way he had been. Gunned down for no reason. It just wasn't right, they all said. But Lamar didn't want to talk. He didn't want to talk at all. All the glowing accolades wouldn't bring his Gramps back. And that was what he wanted more than anything: his grandfather back.

As the conversations continued, Lamar walked slowly out into the front yard and sat on the wooden bench his father had built. He wanted to think about his grandfather in quiet solitude. Remember him. How he looked. How he talked. How he walked. How much he loved his Gramps.

Again, he wished it were all a dream. He closed his eyes tightly and prayed that his grandfather's death had been a mirage, something unreal, an optical illusion. The dream would end and his Gramps wouldn't have been shot and killed. His grandfather would appear with a smile on his face, driving up in his blue Chevrolet to pick him up for another visit. He would sit his grandfather down and interview him for his documentary. He closed his eyes even tighter, wishing, hoping for a dream.

"You're praying or something?"

The voice startled him. He opened his eyes and saw T.C. standing in front of him.

"Naw. I was just thinking about Gramps," he responded. "I didn't hear you come up."

"I was quiet 'cause I thought I saw you praying."

T.C. sat next to his best friend. The sadness on T.C.'s face was apparent, too. For a while, he just sat next to Lamar and stared at the ground, sometimes sneaking a peek at him. He couldn't think of anything to say. He couldn't think of anything to do. Suddenly, angrily, he banged his knee with his right hand.

"That's some messed-up stuff, killing your granddad like that," he yelled out, rising from his seat. "And that White man saying your granddad tried to shoot him! No way. It's a lie! That's so messed up! That's so messed up!"

T.C. sat back down again. He didn't know whether the spontaneous outburst had made things worse. At least he had done something. He had expressed the outrage he felt.

The two longtime friends were silent again. Like everyone else in their community, they were trying to comprehend the incomprehensible—the senseless loss of another Black life.

"They say there weren't no witnesses," T.C. finally said, kicking a pebble with his foot. "So it's just that White man's word. You know how this will go down."

"He ain't gonna get away with killing Gramps!" Lamar jumped up from the bench and thrust a fist into the air as if he were hitting a menacing foe. "He just ain't!"

"I'm with you, Lamar," T.C. assured him. "We should call Reverend Al or that lawyer that represented George Floyd's family. I forget his name."

Suddenly, a patrol car pulled into the driveway. Sergeant Ford emerged and walked toward Lamar and T.C.

"Is Mr. Phillips home?" he asked.

"He's inside," Lamar answered after a long moment.

"Can you ask him to come out here?" Sergeant Ford said. "I don't wanna disturb all those people."

Lamar walked quickly into the house and returned with his father. Sergeant Ford escorted Lamar's father to his patrol car and the two got inside.

Lamar wondered, *What does Sergeant Ford want?* When he looked up, he saw Kyra dash from the house and rush to the car.

"Let's check it out," T.C. suggested to Lamar.

"Dad and Kyra got it," Lamar answered.

They watched as Kyra leaned against the car so she could hear what was being discussed. Suddenly, in a quick motion, she slammed her hand against the car so hard Lamar was afraid she had broken it.

"It ain't going down like that!" Kyra yelled. And she kept yelling it, each one growing louder. "It ain't going down like that! It ain't going down like that! It ain't going down like that!"

Those inside the house rushed out to see what was happening. Ms. Thurmond, the wife of the pastor of the Phillipses' church, ran to Kyra.

"What's wrong?" she asked, placing a comforting hand on Kyra's shoulder.

"They released that murderer!" Kyra yelled. "They let him go. They questioned him and let him go!!"

Soon, Lamar's father exited the car and Sergeant Ford drove away, getting a last look at the people gathered in the Phillipses' yard.

"Sergeant Ford says they had to let the man go 'cause they have no evidence to arrest him," Lamar's father told them. "The man said Papa came at him with a tire iron and he shot in self-defense."

"When Sergeant Ford first came here to tell us about Gramps, he told us the man said Gramps had a gun," Kyra shouted. "Isn't that what he told us? Now it's a tire iron?"

"Well, now he says it was miscommunication. He said two sheriff's deputies investigated the incident and wrote up a report. He said his department didn't have anything to do with it since it happened outside of town. The main issue is that they're saying there was no witness. It's just that White man's account. Sergeant Ford said they did find the tire iron on the ground near the car."

"Give me a break. Of course they found a tire iron. We've got to get a lawyer, Daddy. We can't let it go down like this!"

"We will, Kyra. We will," he told his daughter.

"Lord, we've got to pray. We've got to pray," Mrs. Hall, one of the Phillipses' neighbors, lamented, wringing her hands.

"We've got to get in the streets," countered Mr. Simkins, another neighbor, "if we want justice."

While everyone made their way inside the house again, Lamar and T.C. remained outside. They didn't say anything. Nothing made sense.

CHAPTER 10

The long, arduous day was almost over. Neigh-bors and coworkers had gone. So had church members. It was just the extended Phillips family, all gathered around the television to watch the ten o'clock news. Lamar's uncle Robert and his family were there. So were his aunt Eloise and her daughter, Monica. Lamar's mother's only sister, Myra, had come, too.

But Lamar was still in a fog. He just found it difficult to accept his grandfather's death. Very little interested him. Not even his camcorder. He sat on the sofa holding a family photo album that held two photographs of Gramps. He looked at one for a while, then at the other, and back to the first one again.

When the news began, they didn't have to wait long

for the story about Gramps's killing. It was the lead. A hush fell over the room.

"This is News at Ten, with Andrea Alleman," said the announcer.

"We start the news this evening with a story that has rocked the area," the blonde-haired news anchor said. "A minor traffic accident earlier this morning has led to the death of an elderly Black man from Morton. Drayton Wilkerson has the details. Drayton."

"That's right, Andrea. I'm here in Morton just outside the local police department," Drayton Wilkerson began, looking directly into the camera. "Here is what we know so far. A Black man in his seventies, identified as Joshua David Phillips, and Rutherford Thigpen, who is White and also in his seventies, were involved in a traffic accident earlier this morning on Highway 76 between Thomasville and Morton. Apparently, Mr. Thigpen rearended Mr. Phillips's car. When the two men exited their vehicles, Mr. Phillips became irate and walked back to his car, picked up a tire iron and started toward Mr. Thigpen. Fearing for his life—again, I must repeat, this is Mr. Thigpen's account—Mr. Thigpen ran to his car and retrieved a gun he carried in the glove compartment and shot Mr. Phillips three times in the chest. Mr. Phillips was rushed to Morton General Hospital, where he died. Mr. Thigpen was taken into custody but was later released.

According to authorities, no charges are pending. There are no eyewitnesses so far.

"Mr. Phillips was a community activist in Morton and was one of the leaders of the Civil Rights Movement there during the 1960s. He was also a Vietnam veteran. Mr. Thigpen is a retired businessperson who held various political positions in the town during the 1980s and 1990s. Authorities here told us they are still investigating, but members of the Black community say they are suspicious. Some are comparing the death of Mr. Phillips to the killing of Ahmaud Arbery, who was jogging when confronted, shot and killed by three White men in Georgia, and George Floyd, who was killed by a White police officer in Minneapolis, Minnesota.

"Because the incident occurred outside Morton town limits, it will be investigated by the parish's sheriff's department. We'll stay on top of this, and if there is any breaking news, we'll get back to you. For WKCU News 6, this is Drayton Wilkerson reporting. Andrea."

No one said a word as they sat or stood, trying to digest what they had just seen and heard.

There is something about seeing an incident, an event, on television that renders it factual, complete and final, Lamar thought. *And there it is, the death of Gramps made real and permanent on the television screen. The morning newspapers will provide the last word.*

"We've gotta get a lawyer right away," Uncle Robert advised in a stern voice. "If we don't, this will be swept under the rug. If I remember correctly, Thigpen used to be head of the Ku Klux Klan here in the parish. Papa led a picket of his family's store back in the sixties. I thought Thigpen was dead."

"I thought he was dead, too," Aunt Eloise added. "Those old racists live forever."

"I know a good lawyer in Thomasville," Uncle Robert continued. "Y'all want me to get in contact with him?"

"Is he really good, Uncle Robert?" Kyra wanted to know. "Does he have experience with situations like this?"

"Yes, he's been around for more than twenty years. He has a lot of experience."

"Go ahead and contact him," Aunt Eloise told her brother. Lamar's father nodded in agreement.

"I'm going to see the mayor about this, too," he told everyone. "There should be something he can do."

"What can he do?" Aunt Eloise asked dismissively. "He ain't got no power."

"He has to step up, Eloise. He has to," Lamar's father said determinedly.

"I think you'd be just wasting your time, Lamar," Uncle Robert warned.

"I'll find out, because I'm definitely going to see him,"

Lamar's father responded defiantly. "I've known him for years."

"Listen, everybody. Before we go any further, we should have prayer," Lamar's mother interjected. "We got to say a prayer for Papa. We've been focusing so much on the killer, we've forgotten about him. We need to thank God for his life and all that he meant to us. Let's do that, all right? Let's pray."

They formed a circle in the center of the room, held hands and closed their eyes. The moment was too much for some, as tears began to flow down their faces. Some stood motionless. Others trembled. Lamar trembled, too, as images of his grandfather flashed before him.

"Lord, we come to you at a troubling time," Lamar's mother began. "Our hearts are heavy with grief. We have lost someone that we love so much. But you have said in your Word that you will never leave us or forsake us. So, we need you now, Lord. We need you like never before, God. First, we want to thank you for the life of our father, our grandfather, our friend. He lived a good life. A meaningful life. A life that made a difference in so many ways. And we know he loved you, Lord. We will miss him. But we know he is up there with his dear Ella. As we mourn him, Lord, we ask you to make plain what happened to him. We want to know the truth. Father, we know we can't get through this tough time without you. So be with us, we pray. Help us make it through. Hold all of us in the palm of your hand. And give us your peace that passes all understanding. We need you, Lord. We need you! We need you! Amen. Amen. Amen."

When the prayer ended, everyone was crying. Everyone. Lamar's dad. Uncle Robert. Everyone.

They were remembering their father's and grandfather's generous heart, his love for them, his desire for justice, wishing he was still with them. Realizing, too, that their lives would never be the same without him.

CHAPTER 11

"The mayor's office is on the second floor," Lamar told his parents and his sister after they entered the town hall building. "We got to take those stairs over there 'cause the elevator ain't working."

"How do you know?" Kyra asked.

"I came here with Gramps for a council meeting. I videotaped it."

"And you didn't tell anybody?" Kyra continued with her questioning.

"I forgot."

"Lamar, this isn't the first time we've been here," Lamar's dad said. "We know where to go."

After reaching the second floor, the family saw a sign on a door that read OFFICE OF THE MAYOR and walked toward it.

"I'm wondering what the mayor can do, too, Daddy," Kyra told her father.

"He has influence," he replied. "Why is he in office if his voice doesn't mean anything?"

"It won't hurt," Lamar's mom added. "You never know."

"How y'all doing this morning?" the secretary greeted them when they entered the mayor's office. "I'm so sorry about your loss. I knew Mr. Joshua. He was such a good man."

"Thank you, Clara," Lamar's dad responded. "We appreciate it."

"You're a young lady now," the secretary told Kyra. "I remember when you were taking music lessons with my daughter April. And look at little Lamar, Jr. You're sure growing."

Lamar forced a smile. But he was thinking, *Little Lamar? She had to go there. Well, at least she didn't call me Junior.* That would have really gotten to him.

"Is the mayor in?" Lamar's dad asked. "We'd like to talk with him."

"Yes. Let me tell him you're here," the secretary replied, picking up the telephone receiver.

"Mayor Johnson, the Phillips family is here to see you. Yes, sir." She hung up the phone. "You can go in," she told the Phillipses.

Mayor Johnson met them at the door.

"Come right in. Come right in. I'm so happy to see all of you." He shook Mr. and Ms. Phillips's hands and smiled at Kyra and Lamar.

"You certainly have my condolences and the condolences of the entire town," he continued. "Believe me, my heart is broken. Mr. Phillips was a great man. He did so much for Morton. He was in my office just a few days ago. We had a very productive meeting. Have a seat," he offered. He pointed to two chairs near the window and two near his desk. "Have you set a date for the funeral?"

"No, we haven't," Lamar's dad answered. "It's early yet." No one accepted the mayor's offer to sit.

"You sure you don't wanna have a seat?" He extended the offer again.

"Thank you. But we don't have a lot of time. We wanted to come here to speak with you about what happened to my father."

Lamar's dad stared directly at the mayor, anticipating his response.

"All of us are devastated about what happened," the mayor replied, moving closer to the chair behind his desk.

"Well, Mayor, we are concerned because our father is

being portrayed as a criminal. Quite honestly, we don't believe he attacked Mr. Thigpen with a tire iron. In fact, we were first told our father had a gun, and that's why Mr. Thigpen shot him. Then it was changed to a tire iron. My father was not a violent man. He was *not*."

"Mayor Johnson, my father is being polite about it," Kyra jumped in. "That White man is lying! He killed our grandfather. That's what happened. He shot and killed him for no reason. No! I take that back! He killed him because he was Black. You may be the mayor, but you're Black, too. We don't have to tell you how racism works!"

"Kyra Phillips!" their mother called out loudly. The way she placed emphasis on Kyra's full name meant she was serious. Kyra took a step back.

"Mayor, I apologize for my daughter's behavior," Lamar's mom said.

"I understand, Ms. Phillips. Believe me, I understand. I am sure you know that the incident took place outside our jurisdiction. But we have talked with the sheriff's office to let them know we want to be involved in the investigation. I have ordered the chief of police not to leave any stone unturned in investigating the shooting. I want the truth to come out. The problem so far is that there isn't an eyewitness. There's only Mr. Thigpen's version of what happened. But the chief knows that the investigation can't stop there. They're talking to people who normally drive that way to work, hoping someone may have seen something."

"Can the chief of police be trusted?" Kyra jumped in again. "Does he know the man who shot my grandfather? Mayor, you know in a small town like this, people know each other. They attend the same church and belong to the same organizations. Some of their relationships go back for generations. When you were elected, the chief of police had already been in office for years."

Lamar's mother put her arm around her daughter and walked her to the door.

"We're gonna get justice, Kyra!" Lamar promised his sister. "We just gotta keep fighting like Gramps would," he added as he watched his mother firmly escort his sister out of the office.

Mayor Johnson moved a few steps closer to his desk, searching for a way to escape the awkward moment. He knew that Lamar and his father were watching him closely.

"I don't know what to say," the mayor said, sounding flustered. "All I can do is tell you emphatically that I will do all I can to make sure justice is done for your father. I wish I could make policies to change the hearts and minds of people," he said more to himself than to Lamar's dad. "But I can't. All I can do is work as hard as I know how to make change wherever I can. It's frustrating for me. This is my second term in office. When I was first elected, I thought I could turn things around quickly. But that was a dream. I didn't realize how limited the power of the mayor of this town is."

Lamar's dad extended his right hand to the mayor, who accepted it.

"Listen, Herman," he told the mayor as the two men shook hands. "I know we can trust you. We just want you to do all that you can to make sure things are handled right."

"I promise you that, Lamar," the mayor responded with a smile of relief.

"And, Herman, we know you're doing the best you can," Lamar's dad added. "Just make sure you stay on top of this. You got to stay on top of this."

Mayor Johnson nodded in agreement.

"I'll be there, just like I was when I opened those holes for you on the football field," the mayor told his old teammate.

"Couldn't have made those runs without you," Lamar's father replied. "We had a good team. State champions."

"Yeah. Two years straight. But that was a long time ago, wasn't it? You know, Lamar, when I first heard about the shooting and the details, I said, 'Oh, God, no!' This is bad. A citizen getting killed is always bad. But a White man killing a Black man while a Black man is in the mayor's office! I wanted to holler."

"You didn't pull the trigger, Herman."

"I know, Lamar. I know. But you must realize that the district attorney is the one who decides whether to bring charges in a case."

"I wanna let you know that we're getting a lawyer. It's too big for us."

"Do that. That's what you should do," the mayor said encouragingly. "I will not be offended at all."

"Thank you, Mayor, for your time," Lamar's dad told his high school gridiron mate, going back to formalities.

"I'm glad y'all came by. I hope your daughter is okay."

"This is a tough time for all of us, Mayor."

"I know that, Lamar. I know that."

Mayor Johnson escorted Lamar and his dad to the door.

"This young man here came to our last council meeting," he said. "Mr. Joshua was so proud of him, watching him videotape that meeting. He had a big smile on his face the whole time."

That seems so long ago, Lamar thought.

"God bless you, Mayor Johnson!" Lamar's mom yelled from the outer office, where she and Kyra waited. "We'll keep you in prayer!"

"Thank you, Ms. Phillips. Thank you. I need prayer."

"We all do, Mayor," she added. "We all do."

CHAPTER 12

Lamar was restless. It was Saturday and Gramps's homegoing celebration was just a few hours away. It didn't seem like five days had passed since his grandfather's death. The family had been so busy preparing for the funeral, they didn't have much time to grieve. Lamar didn't realize how much it took to prepare for a funeral. There was always something the family had to look into or approve. In fact, Lamar's mom, dad and Kyra had gone to the funeral home to address another issue that had arisen. Lamar hadn't wanted to go. So he paced the living room floor waiting for them to pick him up. Dressed in a black suit and tie he didn't like to wear, he remembered how much he didn't like funerals. The last one he'd attended was his Grandma Ella's.

A hard knock at the door got his attention. When he answered it, a tall, dark-skinned man who seemed to be about his grandfather's age stood before him.

"Are your parents home?" he asked.

"No, sir," Lamar answered. "They had to go to the funeral home. They'll be back soon."

"I wanted to come by to offer my condolences. Are you related to Mr. Joshua Phillips?"

"Yes, sir," Lamar told the stranger. "He is, well, he was my grandfather."

"I'm Abraham Lumberton. I knew your grandfather. We were in Vietnam together. May I come in?"

Lamar had forgotten his manners. His parents had always taught him and Kyra to be courteous to others.

"You sure it's okay for me to come in?" the stranger asked.

"I think so," Lamar answered, and held the door open for the man.

Once inside, the stranger surveyed the room for a moment. Then he rubbed his rough, weather-beaten hands together and looked away.

"I owe my life to your grandfather. If it weren't for him, I wouldn't be here today. We were in the war together. . . . Vietnam."

"Gramps never talked about Vietnam," Lamar told the

stranger, now interested in what he had to say. "Are you from around here?"

"No. No. I'm from Mississippi. Your grandfather and me were like brothers while we were in Vietnam. Neither one of us wanted to be there. But we had no choice. They were drafting Black men like crazy. Poor White boys, too. Between the two of us, we didn't know enough to get ourselves out of a wet paper bag, being country boys and all."

He slapped his hands together as he remembered. His full-throated laughter followed and echoed throughout the room. Lamar paid close attention to him. This was a part of his grandfather's life that he knew nothing about.

"There was a lot of racism in Vietnam, just like there was back in the States," Mr. Lumberton continued, a pained look on his face. "White soldiers brought their racism with 'em. So us Black soldiers stuck together. We had to."

Suddenly, he broke into a smile.

"We called your grandfather Nails. Yeah. That's what we called him, Nails. That was 'cause he held everything together. He was a leader."

Mr. Lumberton finally stopped talking. "I don't wanna burden you with my story. But when I heard that

Nails had been killed, I had to pay my respects. I live in Jackson, Mississippi, now. I was driving to Dallas when I heard the news on my car radio."

"Can I get you some water or something to drink?" Lamar asked.

"No, I'm fine." Mr. Lumberton kept talking about the old days. "They used to call me Jumping Jack back in 'Nam." He shook his head and started that full-throated laugh again. "I had a chip on my shoulder you wouldn't believe back then. I would be ready to fight at anything. Anything I thought was a slight, I jumped at. That's why they started calling me Jumping Jack. Nails helped me to calm down. He helped me see things different. More clearly.

"I wanna go to the funeral, but I'm not dressed. But I'm hoping it'll be okay. Are they still saying Nails tried to attack that man?"

Lamar nodded.

"That's not the Nails I knew. You know, we've made progress since 'Nam, but there is so much more that needs to be done. Racism is like a heavy cloud of thick smoke that keeps hovering over us. It just won't go away. It just won't."

A beeping car horn interrupted them.

"That's my folks," Lamar told Mr. Lumberton. "I'll

introduce you to them. They'll be glad to meet someone who was a friend of Gramps."

"I'd like that," Mr. Lumberton responded. "I'd like that."

The two walked out, and Lamar locked the door behind them.

CHAPTER 13

Friendship Baptist was one of the oldest Black churches in Morton. The faithful congregation had constructed a new building more than ten years ago. Lamar's parents had grown up in Friendship. Lamar's mom sang in the choir and served as president of the Women's Ministry. Gramps was a member there, too, but he hadn't attended much in recent years.

Three limousines pulled up in front of the church. Inside the sanctuary, Reverend Thomas Thurmond greeted the family as the church organist began playing "We're Marching to Zion." Lamar remembered it was the same hymn that was played at Grandma Ella's funeral.

Aunt Eloise, the oldest of Joshua Phillips's children, and her daughter, Monica, led the family down the aisle toward the front of the church. Lamar's family followed, then Uncle Robert and his family and Uncle Rich and his family.

Reverend Thurmond recited passages from the Bible in a steady rhythm as he led the processional to his grandfather's casket.

"Let not your heart be troubled: ye believe in God, believe also in me (John 14:1).

"In my Father's house are many mansions: if it were not so, I would have told you. I go to prepare a place for you (John 14:2).

"And if I go and prepare a place for you, I will come again, and receive you unto myself; that where I am, there ye may be also (John 14:3).

"And whither I go ye know, and the way ye know (John 14:4).

"Thomas saith unto him, Lord, we know not whither thou goest; and how can we know the way (John 14:5)?

"Jesus saith unto him, I am the way, the truth, and the life: no man cometh unto the Father, but by me (John 14:6)."

A few pews away, Lamar spotted Mr. Lumberton and was glad he had found a seat. T.C. and his family were seated, too. T.C. waved to Lamar when he thought he had gotten his attention. Little John and his family were there, along with Mr. Deloria and Ms. DuBois, the vice principal of Morton Middle School, and their families. Even Ciara and her family sat on a pew behind them. It seemed as if every Black person in Morton had come.

Slowly and methodically, the procession moved forward. Staring straight ahead, Lamar thought it would take forever to get to their seats. He could see his grandfather's casket atop the bier that held it. Each step brought him closer to it.

He could see the pulpit from which the pastor preached positioned directly behind the casket but elevated higher. Another raised, carpeted section held the choir, whose members wore white and blue robes. During most other services, Lamar's mother would be singing with them.

After reaching the front of the church, the pastor went to the pulpit, where he continued to recite scripture. The church officials who had followed him went to their designated area.

When Aunt Eloise and Monica reached the casket, Lamar could hear his aunt weeping softly. Monica put her arms around Aunt Eloise and helped her into the first row of pews that had been reserved for the family. Lamar's parents now faced the casket. Lamar knew it would soon be his turn to stand in front of it.

I don't wanna see Gramps like this, he thought. *I wanna remember him the way he was the last time I saw him, laughing and happy. He was so excited about me doing a documentary on him.*

When Lamar's parents moved slowly away from the

casket, he and Kyra were next. Lamar froze. He couldn't move. His feet were cemented to the floor. Kyra grabbed his hand and led him forward. Lamar closed his eyes and kept them closed as the two stood facing their grandfather. But something urged him to open them because this would be the last chance he would have to see his Gramps.

Lamar squeezed Kyra's hand tightly, and she responded by holding his hand even more firmly. He gritted his teeth and forced his eyes open. There before him was his grandfather, dressed in his black suit and tie, his arms folded across his chest. A United States flag was draped over the bottom half of the casket.

The body looks just like the man I had grown to admire so much, Lamar thought. *The man who had been the pillar of our family, the bedrock, the OG.*

He breathed deeply as tears began to roll slowly down his cheeks. He stood in front of the casket and viewed his grandfather one last time until Kyra gently led him away. When they sat next to their parents, Lamar's mom reached over and squeezed her son's hand tightly.

Lamar was in a daze for most of the funeral. Everything that took place went right past him. The choir sang beautiful hymns. Powerful prayers were prayed. Insightful scriptures were read. People said wonderful things about his grandfather. The mayor spoke and presented a proclamation from the town. The congressperson from their district talked about how Gramps had helped him with his campaign. Even a few White citizens from Morton shared kind words about Joshua Phillips. It all meant little to Lamar. That was, until Reverend Thurmond, dressed in a black robe, stepped up to deliver the eulogy.

Lamar had heard the tall man with the big Afro like from the old days preach many times before. Sometimes Lamar listened. Other times he tried hard to keep from falling asleep. But when the fiery minister stated the subject of the eulogy and the scripture, he got Lamar's attention.

"A man for his time!" Reverend Thurmond thundered. He then began talking about the kind of life Gramps had lived . . . a life of purpose. Lamar listened carefully as the pastor described how his grandfather had stepped up to change things during the 1960s when life for Black people in Morton was determined by Jim Crow laws and customs. He thought about his video camcorder but knew filming wouldn't be appropriate. Not at his grandfather's funeral.

"When most Black people were afraid, although just a teenager, Joshua Phillips answered the 'call of his time,'" Reverend Thurmond informed those who had come to celebrate him.

"Brother Phillips risked his life, but he knew his cause was just. He also knew if not him, then who? Who would fight against the evils of racism, segregation and second-class citizenship imposed on Black people? If not him, who? Who would it be? We owe so much to Brother Phillips and to those like him who fought to open doors and break down barriers for all of us. We must never forget. He was a civil rights leader. He was a Vietnam veteran. He was a devoted husband, a loving father, a doting grandfather. He was one of the first Black postal workers in Morton. He was a freedom fighter!"

The perspiring minister stopped for a moment, grabbed a handkerchief from atop the pulpit and wiped his face. Then he continued.

"Many of you here today didn't know what a hero Brother Phillips was. You're just finding out. And that's our fault. We are too quick to move on. And in doing so, we leave people and much of our important history behind. Brother Phillips was a man of his time. But do you know what? His time was always now, the present. He spent most of his life fighting to make life better for everyone. I ask you, all of you, what are *you* doing? Are you trying to make things better for others?"

After waiting to let his question resonate, he again wiped the perspiration from his face, then looked right, left, and straight ahead. He took a deep breath.

"We don't know what happened on that highway to Thomasville almost a week ago," he began again. "We will find out, however. We will not rest until the truth is revealed so justice can prevail. But we did know Brother

Phillips. We knew what kind of a person he was. We knew his character. The man who has been described by the person who shot him is *not* the Joshua Phillips we knew and loved."

The church vibrated with applause as people stood to acknowledge the pastor's words. But that was not what Reverend Thurmond wanted. He waved his hand for them to be seated. He continued.

"I got to know Brother Phillips soon after I moved here to pastor this church. We talked many times about the problems the people in Morton faced. He was a caring man. He loved his people. No, he didn't believe in sugarcoating anything. He thought whatever the issue was, whatever the challenge, it should be faced squarely, directly. No short-cuts for Brother Phillips. I came to understand that Brother Phillips was that way because he cared so much.

"Joshua Phillips was a man for his time! Are *you*? Are you a person for your time? As we lay this fighter for freedom, this hero, this servant, to rest, I want you all to think about that question. Are you a person for your time?"

Reverend Thurmond sounds a little like Gramps, Lamar thought. *No. A lot like Gramps. Reverend Thurmond tells it like it is, too. Maybe some of Gramps's ways of thinking rubbed off on him during those times they talked.*

When Reverend Thurmond finished the eulogy, two soldiers marched slowly from the back of the church.

When they reached the front, one played "Taps" on his trumpet while the second soldier stood at attention. When he had finished, the two soldiers took the flag from the casket, folded it very carefully and gave it to Aunt Eloise. Lamar looked back just in time to see Mr. Lumberton finish a military salute.

Following the burial at a cemetery thirty minutes away, everyone returned to the church's fellowship hall. Plates piled with food sat in front of the Phillips family, but no one was able to eat. They were too busy talking to all the people who offered condolences and support. Lamar wasn't hungry anyway.

He was relieved when, finally, the family could leave the church. As soon as he returned home, Lamar went directly to his room. He wanted to be alone. He lay across his bed, images of his grandfather racing through his mind. Finally, he fell asleep.

A short while later, Lamar felt a hand on his shoulder. When he opened his eyes, he saw his mother standing near the bed.

"I know you're real sad, Lamar," his mother told him. "You miss Gramps. We all miss him. But I don't think he would want us to be sad. I think he would want us to go on, because we have to go on. After Grandma Ella died, he lost his way a little. But he found it and became more involved in the community again. He became that agitator again. Trying to make things better. I think he would tell us to continue with our lives and do our best to make a difference. Reverend Thurmond captured Gramps very well, don't you think?"

Lamar rose slowly and looked up at his mother.

"He sure did, Mom," he answered. "But, Mom, I didn't get a chance to interview Gramps for the documentary I planned to make. He was so excited about being in it."

"You'll find other ways to do it. Good filmmakers are great at finding alternatives when they're faced with a problem. I'm sure you'll find a way, too."

"You think so, Mom?"

"I'm sure you will!" she tried to reassure her son. "It'll be all right," she told him. "It will be all right."

CHAPTER 14

That Monday, two days after Lamar's grand-
father's funeral, he and T.C. started a new school week.
As they hurried up the steps, Mr. Deloria pulled Lamar
aside.

"I'm sorry about your grandfather, Lamar. If there is
anything I can do, or the school can do, let me know.
Okay?"

"Yes, sir. Thank you, Mr. Deloria. And thank you for
coming to the funeral."

"We wanted to support you and your family. The funeral was just last Saturday. If you'd like to take more time
to be with your family, you can go back home."

"I'd rather be at school, Mr. Deloria. When I'm at
home, all I can think about is missing my grandfather. I'd
rather be at school."

"All right. I understand. We have a counselor for any student who needs someone to talk to. If you need to talk, don't you hesitate, you hear?"

"I won't."

"Take care of your friend, Thomas," Mr. Deloria told T.C. before he walked away. "This is the time that he needs you."

"I got him, Mr. Deloria. You know I got him," T.C. answered quickly.

When Lamar entered the building, all the students' attention turned to him. Some came over and told him how sorry they were about his grandfather. In his first class, students still wanted to talk to him.

"We know your grandfather was killed for no reason," said Randy Newton.

"He was killed just like George Floyd and Breonna Taylor," Jean Scott told him.

"My father said things are as bad as they were decades ago," remarked Robert Ray, the boy who sat next to Lamar in most classes. "He says there's more racism in this town than ever."

Their teacher, Mr. Brunson, ordered the students to take their seats.

"Time for class to start," he announced.

"Lamar," whispered Michelle Graham as other students scrambled to their seats. "Some of the kids at the high school are protesting at the courthouse during lunch. They're protesting for justice for your grandfather. Did you know 'bout it?"

"No," Lamar answered, surprised.

He wondered if Kyra was helping to organize the protest. It sounded like something she would do. But why didn't she tell him? He definitely wanted to be a part of anything that meant standing up for justice for his grandfather. Then he remembered that Mr. Deloria had told him he could go home to be with his family if he wanted to. Lamar got an excuse from Mr. Brunson, grabbed his backpack and hurried from the classroom. On his way out of the school building, Mr. Deloria patted him on the back. "Be careful, son."

No one was at home. Lamar went to his room to check out his video camcorder. Everything was working. He returned to the living room and turned on the television just in time to see a news flash on Channel 6. It was the reporter who had been covering his grandfather's shooting.

"We've gotten word that a group is planning to gather in Morton at the courthouse behind me to demand justice for Joshua Phillips, the Black man who was shot and killed following a minor traffic accident a week ago."

Lamar turned up the volume.

"No charges have been filed against the White man who is accused of shooting Mr. Phillips. His name is Rutherford Thigpen. Mr. Thigpen claims he shot Mr. Phillips in self-defense after Mr. Phillips came after him with a tire iron. Some Black citizens say that Mr. Phillips was murdered and that there is a cover-up. They say they are demanding justice. A group led by students from Morton High School and several local ministers is expected to start assembling here at noon. We'll stay on top of the story and will get back to you with any new developments. This is Drayton Wilkerson reporting from in front of the Morton courthouse for WKCU News 6."

Lamar wondered, *Is this going to be like what happened after George Floyd was killed by those White police officers?*

All over the country and around the world, people marched and called for justice for George Floyd. Television networks, cable and radio stations, newspapers, magazines and social media covered it all. Basketball players, movies stars and even a lot of White people joined the call for justice. Nothing would have been done about it if Darnella Frazier, a teenage Black girl, hadn't videotaped the incident with her cell phone. But in Morton, only a few people had protested. Kyra and her friends walked out of their class, but that was about it.

Lamar wished he had been with his grandfather on that last trip that morning. *Maybe I could have recorded everything and then everyone would know what really happened. I could have proved that Gramps didn't attack Rutherford Thigpen with a tire iron. Perhaps I could have prevented Gramps from being killed.* But he *hadn't* been there.

A while later, he picked up his camcorder and hurried to the bus stop. The bus was always late, so he knew he would have to wait. When it finally arrived, he got on the nearly empty vehicle and found a seat.

Once the bus reached the corner of Main and Mt. Pleasant Street in downtown Morton, Lamar jumped off and rushed to the courthouse. On the way, he passed the district attorney's office, the post office and the building that housed the police jury, the governing body of the parish, and its various departments.

A three-story brown brick-and-concrete structure, the courthouse sat about thirty yards from the street on a neatly landscaped square. A long, recently constructed walkway directed visitors to the thirty-five steps that led to the entrance. Built in 1925, it was listed on the National Register of Historic Places.

Lamar didn't see many people. A few went inside the courthouse to conduct business. But that was it. He wondered where everyone was. He looked at his cell phone to catch the time: 11:30. Just as he placed the phone in his back pocket again, it rang.

"Why didn't you let me know you was gonna leave? I would've gone with you." It was T.C.

"Mr. Deloria told me I could go home if I wanted to. You heard him," Lamar reminded his friend. "You know he wouldn't let you go."

"I would have left anyway."

"That's why I didn't tell you, T.C. You would've gotten in trouble."

"Are a lot of people there?" T.C. wanted to know. "All the students at school talkin' 'bout the protest."

"No one is here yet. It's still early. Ain't you supposed to be in class? I know you're not talking on the phone while you're in class."

T.C. laughed. "Come on, Lamar, I ain't that stupid. I'm in the bathroom. I got permission to leave class."

Lamar noticed several people walk up and stand in front of the courthouse.

"I've got to hang up now, T.C. People are starting to come."

"Man, I sure wish I could be there," T.C. complained. Lamar ended the call.

Five people now stood in front of the courthouse. Lamar saw them look around, so he assumed they probably weren't from Morton. Three were White and two were Black. When one of them turned toward Lamar, he could see the name on the front of his sweatshirt. *WSU.* Lamar knew the letters stood for Williams State University, a school about forty miles away. The university had offered Philyaw a scholarship. But Lamar knew Philyaw wasn't going there, because he wanted to attend a school with a big reputation in basketball.

One of the Black students saw Lamar standing with his camcorder and walked over.

"Do you know what time the protest is supposed to start?" he asked. Short and stocky, the student looked no older than Kyra.

He must be a freshman, Lamar thought.

"I think it's at twelve noon," Lamar answered. "At least that's what I heard."

"Do you know who organized it?" the student asked. "We're from the Committee for Social Justice at Williams State," he said, pointing to the other four students, who were now staring at Lamar.

"We heard about what happened here. So we came to help as much as we can. It looks like another Black person is a victim of racism."

Lamar swallowed hard. "He was my grandfather."

"What?" The student froze.

"He was my grandfather," Lamar repeated.

"Hey, guys," the student called to his friends. "Come on over here. This young brother says that the man who was killed was his grandfather."

"What's your name?" one of the White students asked.

"Lamar Phillips."

"We're sorry about your grandfather," the White student offered. "We're here to help make sure that your grandfather gets justice. And we don't want nothing covered up. That's what usually happens."

"So you don't know who organized this?" the short, stocky Black student asked again.

"No. I found out at school this morning. I go to the middle school. All I know is that some students from the high school supposed to be here at lunch to protest. My sister might know. She's always involved in things like this."

"What's your sister's name?" the other Black student asked.

"Kyra Phillips," Lamar answered. Then he saw Kyra walking toward them with a group of her high school friends.

"There she is now!" Lamar shouted. He ran to meet his sister.

"Kyra! Kyra! They're from Williams State," Lamar told his sister, pointing to the college students. "They came here for the protest."

The short, stocky Black guy stepped up again.

"I'm William Jenkins. This is Jennifer McClain, Martha Lane, Fred Carter and Beauregard Tobias. We call him Beau. He's from Morton."

"I'm Kyra Phillips. I'm with the Students for Freedom at Morton High School. You're from here?" she asked Beau Tobias.

"Yeah. I grew up in the north end, on Tibbets Drive," Beau answered.

"You didn't go to Morton High, did you? I don't remember you."

"No. I went to the private school. Jackson Academy."

"Beau is the one who told us about the protest," William said to Kyra. "So, you all organized it?" he wanted to know.

"Yeah, we wanted to get things started as soon as we could. Other people are joining us. A group of ministers got the permit this morning. They're coming, too."

"Yeah. We were wondering if you had a permit," Fred shared. "The authorities can be rough if you don't."

"We know," Kyra agreed. "That's one of the first things we did when we decided to have this protest."

"Well, we're here to assist. Let us know what we can do," William offered, rubbing his hands together as if he was really ready to get started.

"You can grab some of the signs we made," Kyra informed him. "We're going to start gathering soon. We're gonna march from the front of the courthouse to the end of the block and back again. We got until six o'clock. So be prepared for a lot of walking. We chose this location because all the parish officials have offices on this street."

"Man, you sure have it organized," William declared, looking anxious. "We can't wait to get started."

"Well, it was my grandfather that racist man killed."

Lamar had already begun videotaping. From a distance, he saw someone else filming. His camera, however, was much bigger and more high-tech than Lamar's. WKCU NEWS 6 was emblazoned on it. Standing next to the camera operator was the reporter from Channel 6, Drayton Wilkerson.

As twelve noon neared, more students from the high school arrived. People from the town had come, too. Lamar counted more than one hundred people.

A high school cheerleader handed Kyra a megaphone.

"All right, everyone," Kyra shouted. "Time to march. And no throwing rocks or yelling at anyone. Got that?"

"Yeah!" some of the protestors responded. "We got it."

"And stay on the sidewalk," Kyra added. "Don't go in the street."

The students began marching, some carrying colorful

posters Kyra and her group had given them and others holding up posters they had made themselves. The first protest in Morton in more than fifty years had begun.

There were all kinds of posters, large and small, in color and in black marker.

WE DEMAND JUSTICE.
MURDER IS ILLEGAL!
JUSTICE FOR MR. PHILLIPS.
ANOTHER BLACK PERSON MURDERED!

Someone yelled out, "No justice, no peace!" The protestors picked it up, and quickly a chorus belted out the words that had become familiar from other protests. *No justice,* yelled one group. *No peace,* responded another.

And on it went as the protestors made their way down the sidewalk and back.

No justice!
No peace!
No justice!
No peace!
No justice!
No peace!

Lamar videotaped it all, following the protestors as his camcorder rolled. He made sure he captured Kyra, who, assisted by several other organizers, kept the protestors in line. He noticed sheriff's deputies standing near the window of the courthouse. He wondered if they were going to come out or remain inside. They stayed inside.

As the protestors continued to march, Lamar noticed a small group of neatly dressed men approach. He recognized one of them. It was Reverend Thurmond. Lamar assumed they were members of the ministers' group Kyra mentioned. Reverend Thurmond mounted a portable stage, and Kyra handed the megaphone to him.

"Listen! Listen!" he called as the protestors gathered around the stage. "I have some important information I need to share with you.

"For those of you who may not know me, I am Reverend Thurmond, pastor of Friendship Baptist Church here in Morton. I was Brother Joshua Phillips's and his family's pastor. I and the Morton Ministerial Alliance worked with the Students for Freedom at Morton High School to organize this protest. Our group has had an opportunity to speak with the district attorney this morning, and he told us that no charges will be filed against the man who shot Brother Phillips, because all evidence indicates it was self-defense."

Boooooooooooo, came the collective response. Raised fists and other protestations augmented the frenzied reaction.

"You're right! We can't and we won't accept that," Reverend Thurmond declared, raising his voice louder so he could be heard. "We don't believe it was self-defense. And we can't allow them to let this drop. We've got to keep pushing them to do a real investigation. I know they want this to go away. But we aren't going to let it, are we?"

"NOOOOOOOO!"

Reverend Thurmond continued. "Now, you all know that the district attorney is an officer of the parish. He's not a part of the Morton town government. So the mayor and the town council have no say in what the district attorney does or does not do. Not even the police chief here in Morton does."

"So we get screwed again?" someone yelled. "Is that what you're leading to?"

"No, we're not going to let this go," Reverend Thurmond answered quickly. "We're going to keep demanding justice for Brother Phillips. And we will get justice."

"But they're not going to arrest a White man for killing a Black man!" another student shouted. Lamar moved in so he could get a close-up. The cameraman from WKCU stood opposite him.

"When was the last time that happened?" the student continued, his voice getting even louder.

"This will be different," Reverend Thurmond responded in a more determined voice. "We're not going to be alone. We've been receiving calls from all over the country about this case. We even heard from representatives of a famous basketball player. I can't give his name right now. But he offered his support. This is going to be different."

"LeBron James?!" someone shouted. "Must be LeBron."

"Well, it just could be," Reverend Thurmond responded. "But it could be someone else. A lot of Black basketball players have been using their platform to help make change."

"Especially the WNBA! The women players have been leading the way," Kyra jumped in firmly and very pointedly.

"Yes. Yes. Absolutely," Reverend Thurmond seconded. "Now, let's go back to protesting peacefully. Okay? We will get justice."

As soon as Reverend Thurmond stepped down from the makeshift stage, Drayton Wilkerson and his camera operator rushed up to him.

"I'm Drayton Wilkerson from WKCU News 6," the reporter introduced himself. "I'd like to interview you for our evening news."

"Certainly," answered Reverend Thurmond.

"And what church do you pastor?" Drayton inquired.

"Friendship Baptist Church, where Joshua Phillips was a member."

"And your first name is Thomas. Right?"

"Yes, that's correct," Reverend Thurmond answered.

"I'm ready, Victor," Drayton Wilkerson told his camera operator after clearing his throat. Lamar watched intently. He couldn't wait to watch a professional news reporter in action.

"Are we rolling, Vic?"

"Rolling," Victor answered.

"This is Drayton Wilkerson standing in front . . . wait, wait. Let me do that again. I don't like that opening."

After composing himself, the reporter started again.

"This is Drayton Wilkerson reporting for WKCU News 6. I am here in Morton, Louisiana, in front of the parish courthouse, where a little more than one hundred people are protesting for what they call justice for Joshua Phillips. The people who have assembled here, mostly students from Morton High School, don't believe the account given by Mr. Rutherford Thigpen, the man who said he shot Joshua Phillips in self-defense following a traffic accident. The people here say Mr. Thigpen murdered Mr. Phillips. I'm standing with Reverend Thomas Thurmond, pastor of Friendship Baptist Church in Morton. Reverend Thurmond is one of the leaders of this protest, as well as having been Mr. Phillips's pastor.

"Reverend Thurmond, can you tell our viewers why you are here today? What do you hope to accomplish?"

"Well, we want to see the man who killed Joshua Phillips arrested. We believe it was murder."

"But Mr. Thigpen is claiming self-defense, and there are no witnesses." Drayton moved in a little closer to the reverend, anticipating his reply.

"I don't believe that," Reverend Thurmond answered in an unyielding tone. "We don't believe that. And we think there probably are witnesses. There's more to this than what has been revealed so far."

Drayton looked startled. "So you believe there may be a cover-up?"

"That wouldn't be so unusual, would it? Some White people in this town have a history of covering up for other Whites when the victims are Black."

"But Morton has made a lot of strides over the decades, hasn't it? You have a Black mayor and several Black members of the town council. There are Black members of the parish's police jury governing body. Even your police department is integrated. You think the kind of racism of the past still exists in your town?"

Lamar couldn't wait to hear Reverend Thurmond's response. He thought about how his grandfather would have answered that question. Gramps would have given an hour-long lecture about ongoing injustices. What would Reverend Thurmond say? The clear-eyed minister looked directly into the camera.

"What do you think has been going on in this country for centuries? It takes a lot of work to remove the yoke of racism from around the necks of Black people. Electing a few Black people to political office is a drop in the bucket."

"I'm not challenging you," Drayton explained, looking uneasy. "I'm just doing my job as a reporter by asking important questions."

"There's nothing wrong with that. And I'm just doing my job trying to tell the truth. The last few years, some people have been trying to reverse the little progress that has been made."

"So what's the next step for this protest?" Drayton continued.

"We're going to keep putting on the pressure until we get the truth out and Mr. Phillips's murderer is brought to justice."

"Thank you, Reverend Thurmond."

"Thank you."

"As you can see, there is a lot of frustration here in Morton," Drayton said, now turning to face the camera. "A Black man is dead, and Black people and their supporters here believe it was murder. I guess you can say the racial issues that are facing Morton mirror what has been going on around the country. This is Drayton Wilkerson reporting for WKCU News 6."

"That's a wrap," he told Victor.

"Do you want to keep that ending?" Victor asked. "The part about racial issues around the country mirroring what's happening in Morton."

"Yes, I'm keeping it," Drayton snapped back.

"Are you sure?" Victor persisted.

"Yes, I'm sure. It's the truth, isn't it?"

"Just looking out for your interests," Victor told his news-gathering partner as he shrugged and walked away. Drayton Wilkerson walked away, too, surveying the scene for another angle for a story.

Maybe I can interview the pastor, too, Lamar thought. *I wonder if he'll talk to me.* He ran to catch up with Reverend Thurmond.

"Can I interview you, Reverend Thurmond?" he asked sheepishly.

"Are you being a news reporter today, too, Lamar?" Reverend Thurmond asked, eyeing the video camcorder Lamar held.

"Well, sir, I'm doing a documentary."

"A documentary?" Reverend Thurmond repeated.

"Yes, sir . . . on my grandfather. Me and him talked about doing one before he was killed. I just wanna ask you a few questions."

"That's great. Okay, go ahead," Reverend Thurmond replied.

Lamar thought for a moment, wondering what question to ask first. Then he remembered how Drayton Wilkerson had started his interview with Reverend Thurmond.

"I'm Lamar Phillips here at the protest for justice for Joshua Phillips. I'm talking with Reverend Thomas Thurmond, pastor of Friendship Baptist Church and one of the organizers of the protest. Reverend Thurmond, why are you here today?"

Reverend Thurmond smiled and leaned closer to the camcorder.

"That's a good question. I'm here because I want justice for one of my members, Joshua Phillips, who was killed so brutally. He was shot three times in the chest. And I'm here because I'm tired of the way my people are being treated. I'm here because we have to continue to fight for progress. The struggle for freedom and justice is an ongoing one. But one we must undertake unwaveringly."

"Did you know Mr. Phillips?" Lamar asked, trying to look interested even though he already knew the answer.

"Yes, I did. He was a member of my congregation. He was a good man. He was a civil rights hero. He did so much for this town. I just wish we could have recognized him before this tragic incident."

"Thank you, Reverend Thurmond," Lamar told the pastor, ending the interview.

"Thank you, young man," Reverend Thurmond responded in kind. "Great interview. Your grandfather would be proud."

"Your grandfather would be proud," Lamar repeated to himself.

Drayton ain't got nothing on me, he thought.

Emboldened by the pastor's encouraging words, he looked for someone else to interview. He spotted Kyra and dashed over to her.

"Can I interview you?" he asked, not knowing what her response would be.

Kyra gave him a double take, then answered, "Yes. Don't ask me no dumb questions, now, you hear?" she warned.

"Why would I ask you dumb questions, Kyra?"

"I'm just saying."

Lamar ignored his sister and started the video camcorder rolling.

"I'm here at the protest for justice for Joshua Phillips. I'm speaking with Kyra Ayana Phillips."

"Stop. Stop," Kyra interrupted him, waving her hand at the video camcorder. "Why do you have to use my entire name? Just introduce me as Kyra Phillips."

Lamar tried to keep from laughing. But he knew Kyra was just being Kyra.

"Okay. Okay," he said to her. "But that *is* your name."

"Just do what I say, okay?"

He started again. "I'm speaking with Kyra Phillips. She is the granddaughter of Joshua Phillips and one of the organizers of the protest. Kyra, can you tell us why you organized this protest?"

"Yes, I can tell you. Because a White racist shot and killed my grandfather. And if we don't raise hell, nothing will be done about it."

"What's next?"

"What's next! We're going to keep protesting. We're trying to get justice."

"Do you think you'll get justice?"

"We aren't gonna stop until we do. We'll come here every day. We'll even boycott stores like they did during the civil rights days. We're not gonna stop until the truth comes out and that man is arrested and sent to prison for assassinating my grandfather."

Lamar attempted to ask another question, but Kyra raised her hand for him to stop.

"You have enough," she told her brother. "I've got other things to do."

Kyra rushed off and Lamar looked around for someone else to interview. He noticed Drayton Wilkerson speaking with a mostly White group that had gathered across the street. He raced over to see what was happening. The elderly White man that Drayton was interviewing seemed visibly upset.

"They're making something out of nothing," he spat out. "Just like they always do when something like this happens. They ain't nothing but a bunch of troublemakers!"

"So you believe the shooting was justified?" Drayton asked.

"Hell yeah, it was justified. That, that . . . *man* came after Mr. Thigpen with a tire iron. What would you do if you was in his shoes?"

"So you don't think the shooting was racially motivated?"

"Gimme a break. These people see race behind every doggone thing. I've had it up to here. They got their president. They own professional basketball. By God, the mayor of this town is Colored. I'm tired of 'em! Whose side you on? You're White too, ain't you?"

The elderly White man stormed off, ending the interview. Drayton approached another White man, who shook his head no and walked away. Others turned away as well. As Drayton started to leave, a younger White man came up to him.

"Are you going to run that interview?" he asked.

"It's not up to me," Drayton answered. "The folks at the station make that decision."

"I hope they don't run it. That gentleman doesn't speak for all of us. Some of us don't feel the way he does."

"He speaks for me!" another middle-aged White man shouted. "Run it! We're tired of hiding. Run every bit of it!" He stormed away, too. Discouraged, the younger White man moved aimlessly down the street.

Drayton seemed stunned by the candor he had encountered. After watching the younger White man walk away, so did he.

Thinking he might be able to get an important interview, Lamar approached one of the few Whites who remained. An overweight, middle-aged White man dressed in jeans and a blue flannel shirt seemed like a good prospect. Lamar had seen him before and thought his name was Mr. Madlock. Maybe he would remember seeing Lamar.

"What do you think of the protest?" Lamar asked, holding the video camcorder up high.

"Get away from me, boy! Go back over there where you belong and leave us alone!" the man yelled at him, his face turning red with anger. "If you point that camera at me, I'll take it from you and smash it on the ground." After staring menacingly at Lamar, he stormed off like the elderly White man had done.

Stunned, Lamar just stood there. He hadn't expected *that* response. Yes, he had seen the stares from some

Whites when he went downtown, their eyes examining him, assuming that he might be there to steal. He had even heard the N-word, but not spoken directly to him. But in all his twelve years, he had never experienced the in-your-face hatred that he had just encountered.

All kinds of feelings flooded over him. He felt sad. He felt hurt. He felt angry.

Suddenly, a comforting hand rested on his shoulder. An elderly Black man greeted him when he turned around. "You've just experienced real racism, son," the man told him. "Kind of shocked you, huh?"

Lamar didn't respond. He didn't know what to say.

"I saw you come over here," the man continued. "So I thought I'd follow you, just in case. What did you expect after seeing how they responded to that White news reporter? I grew up experiencing that kind of stuff. You've not faced it so blatantly like that. When something like the murder of a Black man by a White man happens, it surfaces again. That's what your grandfather was fighting against. Now, I think you and me should go back where it's safer."

After crossing the street, Lamar went to the steps of the post office, where he could sit and think. He placed his video camcorder on the step next to him and stared at the sidewalk below him.

The noise the protestors made as they continued their

march seemed far away. He wasn't thinking about the protest now.

"Gramps must have put up with a lot back in the day," he said softly. "I see what he was talking 'bout now."

"This is *something*!"

Lamar was surprised to see T.C.

"Look at all these people!" T.C. added.

"What're you doing here? Did you leave school?" Lamar asked, picking up his video camcorder.

"So many students left to come here, Mr. Deloria closed school and told us to go home and to be careful. Everybody's here. Little John. Even Ray. Here comes Ciara now."

Lamar saw his middle school classmates walking up the street.

"I saw Phil over there somewhere, too," T.C. said. "This is BIG, huh? Your grandfather would be proud."

Lamar nodded, but he couldn't stop thinking about the earlier encounter with the middle-aged White man. He knew it would remain with him forever.

CHAPTER 15

"I apologize for not being available sooner," the short man with a shaved head and a thin mustache explained to the Phillips clan later that evening. "I was in California when my office got in touch with me. I came right over here with Robert as soon as I got back."

"Won't you have a seat?" Lamar's mother offered.

"I think I will," Attorney Smith replied. "I am a little tired. Taking a trip by plane is an ordeal these days. You spend so much time rushing through airports and standing in long lines. I understand a protest got underway today?"

"Yes, Kyra and some of the students at the high school and a ministers' association started it," Lamar's dad answered.

"I was there, too," Lamar added proudly.

He wondered if he should tell everyone about the incident with the middle-aged White man. He decided not to. His mom and dad might not allow him to go to the protests anymore.

"We have to talk about that, young man," Lamar's mother told him. "We're not happy that you left school this morning without letting us know."

"But Kyra was there, too," Lamar protested.

"We knew Kyra would be there. The school gave her permission. You can go to the protest, but only after school."

"Aw, man, Kyra must have ratted on me." Lamar sighed. "By the time school is out, I would have missed all the action."

His mother gave him that look. Lamar knew there wasn't anything he could say to change her mind. Her word was final. And he knew he was right not to tell anyone about the incident.

"Have you had the funeral yet?" Mr. Smith asked, moving to another subject.

"Yes," Lamar's father answered. "A few days ago."

"Well, you have my condolences. These wanton murders of Black people just keep occurring."

"So what's the next step, Mr. Smith?" Robert asked pointedly. "What do we do next?"

Kyra had already researched the attorney. He had a terrific record for winning cases. His biggest was helping to get a man released from state prison years after he had been wrongfully convicted. The freed man had spent twenty-five years behind bars.

Lamar thought one of the deacons at Friendship Baptist Church looked like Mr. Smith. The deacon wasn't as smooth and cool as the attorney. Lamar had already decided to interview the attorney for his documentary.

Attorney Smith pulled out a legal pad and addressed Lamar's dad.

"We have to find out if there was a witness or witnesses," Mr. Smith answered. "The highway between Morton and Thomasville is always busy. Someone had to be driving on it when the murder happened. Especially that early in the morning when people are going to work. Right now, there is only Thigpen's version of what happened. And I believe those sheriff's deputies know more than they're saying. I want to talk to the prosecutor. I already have a call in to his office."

"Do you think he'll talk to you?" Lamar's dad asked. "He's already said that a crime ain't been committed. There's no evidence."

"We'll see. I'm hoping that he will think talking to us is the politically expedient thing to do. This case is starting to get publicity. Two national cable news networks have reported on it."

Lamar could tell that Kyra had something on her mind. She started walking back and forth, wringing her hands. Lamar had seen her like that many times before.

"Mr. Smith, do you think we'll be able to find out what really happened?" Kyra asked, finally stopping to pose her question. "In the cases where Black people have actually found justice, there was always a video. If there's no video, nothing happens. We don't have that. We don't even have a witness."

"Well, Kyra, we're still in the early stages. I am hoping that a witness will emerge, that more information will surface. Remember, before Darnella Frazier posted her video on social media, the killing of George Floyd was being swept under the rug. Would the Ahmaud Arbery case have been tried without the video that was finally released and the persistence of his mother and the community? We can't give up and think nothing can be done. We have to keep pursuing justice for your grandfather. We have to keep the protests going."

For the first time in a long time, Lamar saw his sister relax. "I'm so glad to hear that," she told the attorney.

"Mr. Smith, we *will* keep fighting for justice for my father," Lamar's dad spoke up. "But that story about Papa attacking that man with a tire iron has spread everywhere. They're trying to make our father out to be a thug or gangster."

"We'll deal with that, too," Mr. Smith assured them. "We'll set up press conferences on a regular basis to let people know who Mr. Phillips really was. We'll get his story out there. We will not let others control the narrative.

"Now, how are you all doing?" Mr. Smith asked. "You're dealing with a lot. I know you are still grieving."

"We're handling things the best that we can," Uncle Robert answered. "Right now, we just want to get justice for our father. He meant so much to us."

"I'm going to do a documentary about him!" Lamar said.

"Now isn't the time to talk about a documentary," Kyra told her brother, frowning at him.

"A documentary is a good thing," Mr. Smith interjected. "That's a good way to remember your grandfather's legacy. That's very important."

"Can I interview you?" Lamar asked. "Not now, but later?"

"You certainly can. But right now, we have a few important steps to take. I want to have a talk with Reverend Thurmond. He's the head of the ministers' association, isn't he? I saw the interview the television reporter did with him. I want to talk with the pastor to make sure we're all on the same page. I'm sure he has influence in this area."

"We can go to the church right now to see him," Lamar's dad told the lawyer. "I'm sure he's there. He's a good man. A real good man."

CHAPTER 16

The next morning Lamar and T.C. headed to school together as usual. This time, Little John joined them.

"Go directly to the gym," Ms. Harper told them when they entered the school building.

"I wonder what's up?" Little John said.

"Who knows?" T.C. answered.

When the three entered the gym, they were told to sit anywhere, not in their customary sections by grade.

The portable stage had already been set up underneath the large scoreboard. Mr. Deloria assisted one of the school janitors with the sound system.

"What's going on?" Little John asked Lamar and T.C. as they watched Mr. Deloria.

"Why you keep asking us? You know as much as we do," Lamar replied.

Assembly had never been held so early during the school day. Lamar spotted Ciara sitting in the bleachers on the other side of the gym. She was with a group of girls from her class. He waved to her. After hesitating, she waved back, but like she didn't really want to. Lamar looked around, checking out who was sitting together.

I don't see too many White students, he thought. He counted them. There were only three. Thirty-five White students were enrolled at Morton Middle School. He didn't see Jeff.

"Did Jeff come to school last week?" he asked T.C. and Little John.

"He came a few days," Little John answered.

"Hardly any White students came last week," T.C. added. "I guess their parents scared or something."

Finally, Principal Deloria took the mic and looked out at the noisy student body.

"All right, let's come to attention! Let's quiet down!" he ordered.

After waiting for a moment, he repeated his call for attention. As usual, some students didn't listen. Impatient, Principal Deloria demanded that they quiet down for a third time. A few still whispered to each other. Principal Deloria yelled, "I said quiet down!" That got everyone's attention. Principal Deloria rarely yelled.

Lamar remembered when Mr. Deloria came to Morton a little over a year ago. He was the first White principal Morton Middle School had had in decades. The news in Morton was that White members of the school board chose Mr. Deloria because they didn't want to hire another Black principal. Lamar didn't know much about all that. He only knew that he liked Mr. Deloria. Mr. Deloria and Ms. DuBois, the Black vice principal, treated the students fairly and with respect. That meant a lot to Lamar. To the other students as well.

"I called this special assembly this morning," Mr. Deloria addressed the students, "because I think it is important that we remain together as a family here at Morton Middle School." It was now very quiet.

"We all know that our town is facing big challenges," the principal continued. "A terrible incident has happened. A citizen of our town has lost his life. And a protest started yesterday."

All eyes turned to Lamar, who looked away to avoid the stares.

"And that terrible incident seems to be tearing our community apart," the principal went on. "We have been working hard here at Morton to bring students together, to help forge a different and better future for all of you. We don't want to lose the progress we have made.

"I am hopeful that the truth about this terrible incident, whatever it is, will be uncovered, and that justice will be done. As justice plays out, we have a job to do. You have a job to do. We must continue to provide all of you with the best quality education that we can. And you, you must learn as much as you can so that you can be prepared for the future."

Principal Deloria stopped speaking for a moment and looked upward, as if he was searching for what to say. Then he continued.

"While we are at school, during each school day, I want all of us, teachers and students, to focus on the jobs we have been assigned. And those jobs are, for teachers, providing a quality education, and, for students, receiving a quality education. Our motto here at Morton remains the same . . . ONE FAMILY WITH ONE GOAL: THE PURSUIT OF EXCELLENCE."

"Mr. Deloria, what happened to the White students?" an eighth grader stood and asked the principal. Other students started to whisper.

Principal Deloria hesitated before he answered. Again, he looked skyward as if searching for the right answer.

"I think our focus should be on the students who are here," he responded. "We have been reaching out to the parents of the students who have been absent and will continue to do so."

A long, loud chorus of boos greeted the principal's reply.

"Let's not go that route," Mr. Deloria chastised the students. "Let's focus on what we're supposed to do. Okay?

"Now, I know that there is a protest planned for today and, perhaps, for days to come. We respect those who desire to utilize their First Amendment rights. But every day is a school day here at Morton Middle School, and every student is expected to be in school for the entire school day."

"That's not fair."

"We want to join in the protest."

"What about our First Amendment rights?"

The principal allowed the grumbling students to have their say. Then he raised his right hand. The students knew that meant to settle down. A few students didn't.

"All right! All right! This is not the way students at Morton Middle School should behave. Some of you are not showing that true Morton Tiger spirit."

Finally, it was quiet again. The principal took the microphone from the stand and walked toward the end of the portable stage so he could be closer to the students.

"I want all of you to be informed. I want all of you to be concerned about the kind of world we must live in. All of you have a role to play in helping to move our world forward. But right now! Right now! Your responsibility from eight a.m. until three-thirty p.m. is to go to your classes so you can get the best education you can. So, no student will be excused during the regular school day. After school, what you do is the responsibility of your parents. Understood?"

Reluctantly, the students nodded.

"Ms. DuBois, can you make sure the students get to their classes in an orderly manner, please?"

"Yes, sir, Mr. Deloria."

Lamar, T.C. and Little John stood with the other students and moved slowly out of the gym.

"I guess we can't go to the protest," T.C. whispered to Lamar.

"You're not going, are you?" Little John asked Lamar.

"I don't wanna get in trouble," Lamar answered. "I'll go after school is out."

"I guess Jeff went to another school, too, huh, Lamar?"

"I guess so, T.C. I don't want to talk about it."

CHAPTER 17

"**I have to get my camcorder,**" Lamar told T.C. when the school day ended. The two friends raced to Lamar's house, where Lamar picked up his video camcorder and they headed to the protest.

"Wow! There're more people today than yesterday," T.C. said, staring at the large crowd.

"Yesterday was the first day," Lamar replied, clutching his camcorder. "Kyra said more people would come today."

As Lamar and T.C. made their way through the crowd, they noticed that there were more people across the street opposing the protest than there had been the first day. They, too, had signs they held high. Lamar hurried over and began videotaping them. Remembering the incident with the middle-aged White man, he was careful not to get too close. The signs read:

JUSTICE FOR RUTHERFORD THIGPEN!
NO COVER-UP, JUST THE TRUTH!
MAKE AMERICA GREAT AGAIN!
CAN'T TAKE THE TRUTH!
REAL JUSTICE!

A group of men clad in khaki uniforms stood at attention like they were in the military. They stared menacingly at the protestors. Students from the predominately White high school north of Morton were there as well. Some waved Confederate flags. Lamar had seen that flag before, on cars and trucks, and sometimes on poles in the yards of White citizens. But this was the first time he had seen a group of White people protesting with it.

Lamar noticed that something else was different, too. Police officers from Morton and deputies from the sheriff's department formed a long line on the side of the street where those who were protesting for justice had assembled, making sure they remained in the area that had been designated for them. There were no police across the street where the mostly White protestors stood. Every once in a while, members from both groups yelled at each other, screaming insulting names.

Drayton Wilkerson was there taking notes. Other TV reporters had come, too. WXYD and KDKZ were emblazoned on two large cameras. A large WRBZ van was parked down the street in front of the post office.

"They're really mad, huh?" T.C. asked Lamar, watching counter-protestors run toward them while holding up small Confederate flags.

"They sure are," Lamar agreed. "Where they come from?"

Lamar decided to check out Drayton. He hurried to where Drayton stood, typing on his phone.

"Hi," Lamar said.

"Hi yourself," Drayton replied, still focused on his notes.

"I saw you on the news. You did a good job."

"Why, thank you," Drayton replied. "You're recording too, I see," he told Lamar after checking out the video camcorder.

"It's nothing like that big camera your cameraman got," Lamar said.

"Well, you have to start somewhere. You want to be a reporter or a cameraman?" Drayton asked.

"I'm gonna be a filmmaker," Lamar answered. "You know, like Spike Lee."

"Good for you," Drayton told Lamar. "You're certainly getting experience today."

Drayton reached into his shirt pocket and pulled out a business card.

"Here. Hold on to this. Let's stay in touch."

"Wow! Thanks!" Lamar said excitedly as he slid the card into his pants pocket.

"Hey, Drayton," Victor, the reporter's camera operator, called. "We got to get moving."

"On my way," Drayton answered. "See you around," he told Lamar. "I didn't get your name."

"Lamar Phillips."

"Phillips? Are you related to Joshua Phillips? The man who was killed?" Drayton asked, looking startled.

"He was my grandfather," Lamar answered.

"I'm sorry that happened to your grandfather, Lamar. I have to run," he said, starting to move away. "Hold on to my card, okay?"

Lamar watched as Drayton rushed to catch up with Victor.

"I didn't know where you went," T.C. said, walking up to Lamar as Lamar walked back to where the protestors were. "I saw you talkin' to that news reporter."

Suddenly an opened bottle of water crashed to the ground near them. They looked to see where the bottle had come from. But they couldn't tell. A tall, dark-skinned teenager emerged from among the protestors, picked up the bottle and flung it back across the street toward the counter-protestors. The half-empty bottle landed in the street.

"Don't respond!" Reverend Thurmond yelled, rushing over. "You can't do what they do!"

"We're supposed to let them hit us?" the teen yelled back. "We ain't gonna take that crap!"

"We're here to make sure there is justice for Mr. Phillips. We can't let anything get in the way of that," Reverend Thurmond scolded the young man.

"So are we. But we ain't gonna take no violence from no racists!" another student shouted at Reverend Thurmond.

Sensing that things might get out of hand, Kyra grabbed a megaphone and stood on a makeshift stage. Lamar followed, continuing to record.

"Listen up, y'all. That's my grandfather we're fighting to get justice for! I know he wouldn't want us to respond to violence with violence! I don't either! I said this will be a peaceful protest, and it will be. Y'all feel me? I said, y'all feel me?"

"Yeah, we feel you!" someone shouted.

"So, listen, let's check each other. If you see someone next to you doing something that's going to jeopardize our protest, stop them. The least minor thing we do will be turned against us. You all know that. So, let's be cool. Okay? We're making a difference. The fact that we're here in such big numbers is a major statement. Love y'all!!!"

"We love you, too, Kyra!" several high school students shouted.

When Kyra stepped down, Lamar beamed. "That's my big sister."

More water bottles were thrown at them, but no one responded. Several hit police officers and they didn't react either.

"If that was us throwing those bottles that hit them, the police would be all over us," noted T.C.

"You probably right," said Lamar. "I'm going to the other end of the street so I can get some different footage."

"I'm with you," T.C. said.

As they hurried down the street, T.C. spotted Lamar's parents.

"Hey, look, Lamar. Here comes your dad and mom. They got somebody with them."

"That's the lawyer," Lamar informed his friend. "And you know Uncle Robert."

Lamar's parents, Robert and Attorney Smith walked directly to where Kyra and Reverend Thurmond were standing. When Lamar's dad saw Lamar, he waved for him to join them.

"Listen, everyone, I think it's important that we introduce the family of Brother Joshua Phillips," Reverend Thurmond told the protestors.

"Many of you who live in Morton know them. But

we have the media here from out of town, so people from around the country will be getting a chance to meet them for the first time. First, we have Mr. Phillips's oldest son, Lamar, Sr., and one of his other sons, Robert. Lamar, Sr.'s lovely wife, Diana Renee, is also here, along with their son, Lamar, Jr., and their daughter, Kyra. We are so thankful for the leadership that Kyra has provided. She is one of the organizers of this fight for justice for her grandfather."

Reverend Thurmond's recognition of Kyra drew a round of cheers.

"Some of you probably don't know that the Phillipses have an attorney who's helping with this case," Reverend Thurmond continued. "He's from Thomasville, and for years, he has represented people in civil rights cases and otherwise. I think he has just come from a meeting with the district attorney. Let's give Attorney Henry Louis Smith a warm Morton welcome."

Mr. Smith mounted the stage, and he and Reverend Thurmond shook hands as the attorney received a smattering of applause. Lamar was right on it. His video camcorder was now like an extension of him as he moved fluidly from spot to spot.

"Where's Reverend Al and Benjamin Crump? Y'all couldn't get them?" someone yelled rudely. A few in the crowd laughed, but the person who asked the question seemed to be serious. Reverend Al Sharpton and Benjamin

Crump were well-known for helping to fight for justice in Black communities.

"They are both aware of this case and have pledged their support," Mr. Smith answered. "But Reverend Al and Attorney Crump can't be everywhere. There are so many of these kinds of cases. We each have to assume responsibility to ensure that we get justice.

"Now, as Reverend Thurmond said earlier, we have had a meeting with the prosecutor. The prosecutor is responsible for criminal cases like this. He is saying that there isn't any evidence to file charges."

That news didn't go over well. Protestors booed.

"Wait, now! The good news is that what we're doing here is making a difference. We must continue to keep this case before the public. It makes it so much harder for them to sweep this under the rug, which is what I think they would like to do. We are hoping that someone who may have seen the incident will step forward. We believe somebody must have seen what happened. That highway is always busy with cars coming and going between Thomasville and Morton. Even now, I bet someone is trying to muster up the courage to step up.

"We have to continue to protest. Reverend Thurmond has told me that we will be here every day until there is justice for Mr. Phillips. But we must be nonviolent. That's what the family wants. And that's what we must be. We will protest every day, but we will do it nonviolently. I believe Reverend Thurmond and the group have set a regularly scheduled time to gather to protest. Is that right, Reverend Thurmond?"

"Yes, Attorney Smith. We will protest every day from twelve noon until six p.m. We've gotten a permit for those hours from the town. We must not, however, interfere with anyone who has to go into the buildings on this street to take care of business. And at exactly six p.m., we'll depart. We don't want to be here when it turns dark. That's a recipe for trouble."

"Thank you, Reverend. So that means we have under two hours today to continue to express our call for justice for Mr. Phillips and then we will go back to our homes."

Oh, I wish I was in the land of cotton,
Old times there are not forgotten;
Look away, look away, look away, Dixie Land.

The sudden outburst of song from the counter-protestors caught everyone's attention. Lamar looked across the street. The group had gotten even more boisterous, thrusting fists in the air defiantly and clapping excitedly. Others held their posters high and waved their Confederate flags in the air. Led by the men wearing khaki uniforms, they launched into another verse enthusiastically.

In Dixie's Land, where I was born in,
Early on one frosty mornin',
Look away, look away, look away, Dixie Land.

"Y'all know that song?" Lamar and T.C. heard some-one ask. When Lamar looked back, he recognized the man who had come to his rescue the day before.

Lamar and T.C. looked at each other.

"A little," Lamar answered.

"The song is called 'Dixie,'" the man said. "It was the anthem of the Confederacy during the Civil War. It's still important to a lot of White people who hang on to those old days. For most of us Black folks, however, that song, just like that flag they're holding, represents slavery, segregation and discrimination."

Lamar, T.C. and the man listened as the counter-protestors sang the third verse.

I wish I was in Dixie, hooray! Hooray!
In Dixie's Land I'll take my stand
to live and die in Dixie.
Away, away, away down south in Dixie.
Away, away, away down south in Dixie.

When the song ended, that side of Main Street rever-berated with loud cheers, cheers like those at a rap concert or a football game. As they grew even louder, someone from the group protesting for justice mounted the stage and started to sing.

Lift ev'ry voice and sing,
Till earth and heaven ring,
Ring with the harmonies of Liberty

Others joined in. It was the Black National Anthem. Not everyone knew all the words. But those who did sang it proudly and passionately. Lamar knew the first verse because Morton Middle School sang it during Black History Month. He knew it expressed racial pride and hope for the future despite the racism and discrimination that Black people had faced. He joined in. So did Kyra, T.C. and the other students, as the melody rang out.

Let our rejoicing rise,
High as the list'ning skies,
Let it resound loud as the rolling sea.
Sing a song full of the faith that the dark past has
*   taught us,*
Sing a song full of the hope that the present has
*   brought us;*
Facing the rising sun of our new day begun,
Let us march on till victory is won.

Now the White protestors tried to sing louder than their opposition.

Oh, I wish I was in the land of cotton,
Old times there are not forgotten;
Look away, look away, look away, Dixie Land.

But their number was smaller.

Most of those who sang "Lift Ev'ry Voice and Sing" only knew the first verse. They sang it again, this time even louder.

There, on Main Street, in the small town of Morton, two groups of people, all Americans, used songs that were dear to each as weapons, part of a centuries-long struggle that sometimes seemed to have no solution. When the two groups finished singing, they used pointed fingers and hurled epithets at each other. Lamar recorded as much as he could with his video camcorder.

Go back to Africa!
This is our country just as much as it is yours!
No more free rides!
You're getting the free rides!
Where's your white hoods!
You'll see them soon enough!

From a distance, Lamar saw Jimmy Clay and Frankie Pierce with handfuls of rocks, poised to throw them across the street at the White counter-protestors. He dashed over to try to stop them, but he was too late. Several pebbles hit their marks. Chased by police officers, Jimmy and Frankie disappeared among the protestors.

"All right, everybody, we're ending the protest for today!" Reverend Thurmond announced. He had seen the incident, too.

"We have had a full and productive day. But let's make sure we remain nonviolent. We must do that. If you're interested in being a member of the peace-keeping squad, please join us tomorrow morning at eleven forty-five. Make sure all of you go home. Now don't mill about. And make sure you leave in groups. No one should be alone. The devil is busy."

As the protestors departed, so did the counter-protestors. The police maintained their positions, making sure that the two groups remained separated. Lamar, his dad, mom and Attorney Smith made their way to their cars. They had only gotten a few yards when Ray rushed up to Lamar and pulled him aside.

"I'm glad you got your camcorder," he told Lamar.

"Why?" Lamar asked. He knew Ray was always scheming.

"We're going over to Evergreen Street to pull down that statue of that Confederate soldier. You can video-tape it."

Lamar had seen the statue many times before. The Confederate soldier stood erect, atop a marble pedestal, clad in a Confederate uniform. He held a rifle in front of him. The monument was more than twice Lamar's height. Lamar didn't know when it had been built, but he knew it was old. He knew, too, it was one of many such monuments in Morton that honored the Confederacy, those who fought to secede from the United States during the American Civil War of 1861–1865. Those statues had been a part of the culture of the area for decades.

"Why are you doing that?" Lamar questioned, surprised. "I thought you told Gramps you didn't care about Black 'stuff.' That's what you said."

"Man, that old statue should have been pulled down a long time ago," Ray answered with a shrug. "They taking down statues like that all over the country. My ol' man say that thing is all about the slavery days. It'll be fun pulling it down."

"We ain't here for fun, Ray," Lamar spoke up. "We're protesting for justice for my grandfather."

Lamar wondered how many at the protest were like Ray, looking for a good time. There were always people like Ray who caused problems for others who were trying to do the right thing.

"So you ain't coming?" Ray asked defiantly.

"No, I ain't coming," Lamar answered decisively. "You gonna get in trouble."

"Naw, I ain't. Nobody's gonna know about it till it's done. I'm out, dude." Ray hurried down the sidewalk and caught up with Jimmy, Frankie and several other boys from Morton High School. They turned the corner onto Evergreen Street.

Something bad is gonna happen, Lamar thought. *Should I tell Mom and Dad and Attorney Smith? But I don't wanna be a snitch.*

CHAPTER 18

Lamar walked into the kitchen and placed his empty cereal bowl in the sink. His father and mother had already gone to Thomasville to meet other lawyers whose counsel Attorney Smith had sought. Kyra had left for school. His cell phone rang.

"Hey, Lamar, did you hear what happened to Ray?" It was T.C.

"What about Ray?" Lamar asked.

"He's in the hospital. He, Jimmy, Frankie and some other guys tried to pull that statue down. You know, the one on Evergreen. The police ran them off when they first tried, but they went back late last night. A group of Whites tried to stop them, and a big fight broke out. Ray got beat up pretty bad. Others got hurt. Some White people, too. But Ray got the worst of it."

"I should have told somebody they were gonna do that," Lamar said.

"You knew 'bout it?"

"Yeah, he told me."

"Well, too late now. I'm on my way over to your house."

Lamar grabbed his backpack and video camcorder and headed out the door. He knew he wasn't supposed to take the camcorder to school. Mr. Deloria encouraged students to pursue extracurricular activities, but not when they interfered with schoolwork. Lamar thought, *What would Spike Lee do?* He decided he would stash it in his backpack, so that he would have it when he went to the protest after school.

As soon as Lamar reached the bottom step of his house, he saw T.C. coming up the sidewalk.

"Oh! I forgot," T.C. said, preparing to drop more bad news on Lamar. "Somebody set fire to Mt. Moriah Baptist Church last night."

"What?! That's the church on Longfellow Highway?"

"Yeah. My cousins go to that church. The fire department got there, but the sanctuary got burned pretty bad," T.C. said. "People are saying White people did it as payback for that statue. That's wild, ain't it, Lamar?"

"Sure is. What's going on around here? First Gramps is killed and now a church is set on fire."

At school, they were directed to the gym for assembly. Principal Deloria wasn't there. He was always at school. Even when he was feeling ill, he still showed up. But it was Ms. DuBois, the vice principal, who walked to the podium.

"Good morning," she greeted the students. "For those of you who are wondering, Principal Deloria has gone to the hospital to visit a student who was injured last night."

It has to be Ray, Lamar thought. *All that attitude he had when Gramps tried to show him that documentary.*

"Students," Ms. DuBois continued, "for the near future, we will have assembly every morning before classes. All of you are expected to remain in school until the dismissal bell rings. Do not leave this campus! I repeat! Do not leave this campus! And after school, you should go home unless you are with your parents or have gotten their permission to go elsewhere.

"The issues we're facing here in Morton aren't unlike those being faced in other places," Ms. DuBois continued over the buzz in the gym. "But we want to make sure that we at Morton Middle School maintain the culture we have spent months building. We're not where we want to be, but we have made progress. Our motto is still our North Star. And what is it?"

"ONE FAMILY WITH ONE GOAL: THE PURSUIT OF EXCELLENCE," the students responded.

"That's correct. And we will continue to pursue that. Say it again!"

"ONE FAMILY WITH ONE GOAL: THE PURSUIT OF EXCELLENCE."

"Now move quietly to your classes," Ms. DuBois told them. "Follow the directions of the teacher in front of you. And have a great day."

Not much learning took place during the school day. Teachers tried to maintain their regular class routine, but students were too wired about what was happening in their town, the church that was burned and of course, the killing of Joshua Phillips.

After school, Lamar and T.C. ran as fast as they could to the protest. Following last night's incident, Lamar didn't know what to expect. Would people still be allowed to protest? Would there be more counter-protestors?

There were even more people protesting for justice for his grandfather. Some were probably there because the church had been burned. There were more White people who had joined the protest. But more counter-protestors were there as well. A larger contingent of police officers and sheriff's deputies were deployed, too. Their body armor, vests and helmets made them look as if they were ready for a space war. They formed a long line and kept the protestors for justice for Joshua Phillips on their side of the street, near the courthouse. Reverend Thurmond and peace-keeping volunteers walked up and down the line of protestors as they marched.

"Let's not give the police a reason to turn on us!" Reverend Thurmond reminded them. But Lamar could sense that the growing number of counter-protestors alarmed him.

"Let's be cool," he continued to warn his people. "We're here for a righteous reason. Let's not forget that."

"Stay on the sidewalk," Kyra ordered. "Keep marching in line. Don't go into the street. We're supposed to stay on the sidewalk."

Lamar wondered where his parents were. Then he remembered they had gone to Thomasville with Mr. Smith.

A short while later, Reverend Thurmond introduced Reverend Flanigan, the pastor of Mt. Moriah, the church that had been set on fire. The cheers and applause from the protestors were almost deafening as the short, balding, middle-aged minister took the platform. Lamar readied his camcorder and focused in on Reverend Flanigan.

"Praise the Lord!" the pastor exclaimed, almost brought to tears by the way he had been received.

"Praise the Lord!" came the enthusiastic response. Reverend Flanigan gathered himself.

"As most of you know, my church, Mt. Moriah Baptist Church, was set on fire last night and the sanctuary was burned pretty bad. We can't conduct services there now. As y'all know, Mt. Moriah is an old church. According to the fire department, accelerants were placed all around the church and inside the sanctuary. Once the fire was set, it was difficult to stop. We're thankful the church didn't burn down completely."

Still teary-eyed, the minister looked out at the attentive protestors.

"We would have celebrated our seventy-fifth anniversary this September," he told them. "But we're gonna rebuild the sanctuary. The Lord hasn't brought us this far to leave us! We wanna thank all of you for your prayers. We've already started to receive donations. Our sister churches have opened their doors to us. Would you believe a White church reached out to us, too? This Sunday, at three p.m., we will have our regular service at New Revival Baptist Church on Plank Road. I wanna thank Reverend Washington and his congregation for their generosity in making their church available to us. And thank all of you for your support."

People rushed to embrace Reverend Flanigan after he stepped down from the stage.

"This terrible incident is being investigated by the fire department and by the police," Reverend Thurmond said, now addressing the crowd.

"Like they're investigating the murder of Mr. Phillips?" someone from the crowd derided him.

"They'll get away with this, too," someone else shouted.

"That's why we're here," countered Reverend Thurmond. "We're fighting so that they won't get away with it. So, let's continue to stand up for justice! No, it will not be easy. But what alternative do we have?"

A small rock landed near one of the officers. Another one followed, barely missing a second officer.

"Please don't do that!" Reverend Thurmond yelled. "Don't throw anything. We want to remain peaceful. We must remain peaceful."

Quickly, peace-keeping volunteers grabbed the rock throwers and escorted them away. The counter-protestors continued to yell from across the street. Those protesting for justice yelled back. As he kept on videotaping, Lamar wondered how much worse it would get. He knew his grandfather wouldn't be happy with the aggressive antics of some of the protestors.

CHAPTER 19

Lamar was exhausted. On television, protest-ing looked like fun. But he knew now that it was work. And he didn't have to do all that walking like the full-day protestors.

"What're you doing?" Lamar's father asked, entering his son's room.

"Transferring some of the stuff I've videotaped to my computer!"

"Your grandfather knew what he was doing when he helped you buy that camcorder. He was always thought-ful like that, knowing what you cared about. I miss him. I miss him a lot."

Lamar's dad moved slowly toward Lamar's bed and sat down.

"I don't think we'll ever find out what really happened

to your Gramps," he said in a quiet voice. "Another Black life will just be tragically lost, and no one will be held accountable."

He buried his face in his two large hands.

Lamar looked at his father. For the first time, he had expressed hopelessness.

It is going to take everyone fighting for justice for Gramps, he thought. *No one can lose faith or express doubt. Not now.*

He thought about what Gramps had told him that day they'd visited the place where his grandfather was born and raised. *Gramps knew I didn't know that much about Black history, and he was concerned. He said, "It's our fault. Me, your dad, your mom, the school. None of us have done a good enough job sharing the real history of Black people. We dropped the ball. Knowing your history, who you really are, helps prepare you for most anything." I'm beginning to understand what Gramps meant. If I knew more about our history, would I have been so surprised that there are still racists? Gramps was a fighter. I gotta be a fighter, too.*

"Dad, if we keep protesting, if we don't give up—"

"If there ain't a witness who saw what happened, Lamar, all the protesting in the world won't matter," Lamar's dad interrupted. "That man isn't gonna come out and confess that he killed Papa!"

"We can't give up! We can't! Gramps wouldn't give up if he was fighting for justice for one of us."

"I know, Lamar. But your grandfather was someone special. I guess I didn't understand just how special he was."

"Dad, what's wrong?" Lamar asked, realizing that something else was troubling his father.

His father thought for a long moment before he answered. "I've just been thinking a lot since Gramps got killed, son. A lot has been running through my mind."

"Like what?"

"I don't know. A lot of things."

"Like what, Dad?" Lamar continued to probe. He realized this was the first time he had ever questioned his father so directly. But this was a different time. So much was at stake.

"Well, like maybe I haven't done what I'm supposed to do to help you and Kyra make it in this society. That's for starters."

"What do you mean, Dad?" Lamar turned away from the camera and laptop and faced his father.

"I have been so focused on building a life here for myself and my family, you know, working hard and acquiring material things. But I forgot to provide you and Kyra with the kind of foundation you need to make it as Black people in this country. This whole thing with Papa has made me realize that. Sometimes, I guess you close your eyes to things. And when you do that, you can go on like everything is all right. Everything is okay when it ain't. Papa was involved in the community in so many ways. But I have been absent."

"I guess Kyra is just different, huh?"

"I think she's more like your grandfather. You're just learning about Papa's history. I should have been sharing it with you all along. I should have spent time with you like Papa had started to do before he was killed. Me and your mom left it up to the schools to teach things you should know. But that was our responsibility, too. Papa and people like him fought to make things better. They made it possible for me to pursue a better life. But, son, what have I done to make it better for those coming behind me? That's the question Reverend Thurmond asked all of us at Papa's funeral. What are you doing to make things better?"

Lamar had never heard his father speak that way before. His conversations had always been about getting a better position at his job or getting a raise. Sometimes he talked about fishing, a sport he loved or the new car he wanted to buy.

"This town has made some progress, and I've benefitted from it personally," Lamar's dad continued. "I got a pretty good job, and so does your mother. But other Black people don't. There's still a lot to be done to make sure people are treated fairly and have opportunities no matter what color they are or how poor they are. That's what Gramps tried to do—make things better for others, not just for himself. In a way, I have lost connection with my heritage, my past."

"Maybe that's why Gramps took me to his old homeplace. There was no house there. Just land all filled with tall grass and bushes. Maybe he wanted to stay connected to his past."

"When was that?" Lamar's dad asked, his interest piqued.

"A few days before he was killed."

"I know where it is. I didn't know he took you there."

"He talked about how he and his family picked cotton," Lamar told his father, "and that he didn't go to school for real until he was twelve years old, when they moved to Morton."

Lamar's dad stared at the floor for a long moment, then rubbed his eyes with his hands, trying to keep the tears from welling up in them. Then he rose slowly from the bed. "I've got a lot of work to do. A lot. But I know that now."

A knock at the front door interrupted them.

"I got it, Dad," Lamar said, and hurried to the living room. Philyaw stood in the doorway.

"What's up, lil' brother?"

"You, Phil."

"No, it's you."

By now Lamar's dad had walked into the living room.

"How're you, Mr. P.?" Phil greeted him.

"I'm okay, Phil. Come on in."

"Kyra ain't home, is she?" Philyaw asked.

"No, she and her mother went out."

"No news about your father's case yet, Mr. P.?"

"Not yet, Phil. We still have hope, though. We ain't gonna give up."

The remark drew a smile from Lamar.

"Well, if there's anything I can do, let me know. I've been at some of the protests. I was there today."

"We appreciate that, Phil. But you better be careful. You got a lot to lose. You've got all those scholarship offers."

Lamar looked at Philyaw to see how he was going to answer. The basketball star bobbed his head up and down and looked around the room. Then he stared Lamar's dad directly in the eye.

"Mr. P., there are things more important than basketball. I had a lot of respect for your father. He was an OG. I mean, I know the opportunities I got are because people like him fought so hard to make life better for all of us. The least I can do is support the call for justice for him."

Lamar was surprised. He hadn't expected that answer. He thought Philyaw was all basketball. Just a big-shot jock. *It goes to show,* he thought, *that you have to be careful how you judge a person.* He had seen Phil at the protests. But he thought Phil was there just to be near Kyra.

"I appreciate that, Philyaw. I really do," Lamar's dad told Phil. "Yes, my father was a good man."

"No problem, Mr. P."

Phil hit Lamar with a playful tap on the shoulder.

"Be cool, lil' man," he told him. Then he turned to Lamar's father. "You know, Mr. P., you have the next big-time movie director here. I see Lamar at the protests. He's all over the place filming everything."

"You're the one who'll be big-time, Phil," Lamar shot back, sounding like T.C. "You'll be all NBA in a few years."

"I'm trying, dude. Listen, I'll check y'all later. Tell Kyra I dropped by. And, Mr. P., please tell her not to be so hard on a brother. I mean to marry her one day. You know, when we're both ready."

"I will, Philyaw," Lamar's father assured him. "Kyra just likes being tough. But I'm proud of her."

"Me too, Mr. P.," Philyaw said.

"He's *really* a nice guy," Lamar's dad said after Philyaw left.

Lamar headed back to his room to finish downloading. When he checked his computer, there was a new email. But he couldn't identify who it was from. He didn't recognize the email address and there was no subject line. At first, he thought it was a marketing ploy or someone trying to pull a scam. His parents always cautioned him about inappropriate emails. Just as he started to delete it, something told him not to, that he should open it. When he did, he saw in all bold, capital letters the words *IMPORTANT AND CONFIDENTIAL.*

Below it was a link. Again, Lamar thought it might be a scheme to hack into his computer. But again, he got the feeling that he should click on it. The link was to a video. After it opened, he watched it closely. Two cars were parked about five yards apart on the side of a highway. Two men stood between the cars. They seemed to be arguing. The more they argued, the angrier each seemed to get.

One of the cars seemed familiar to Lamar. It looked like Gramps's old blue car. Lamar enlarged the image. *One of the men looks like Gramps,* he thought. Suddenly, the other man, an elderly White man, rushed to his car and pulled something from it. He rushed back to the elderly Black man and pointed the object at him. Three popping sounds followed. The Black man fell to the ground, clutching his chest. Lamar was so shocked, he stumbled over his chair.

Did I just see Gramps get killed?

"DAD! DAD! COME HERE! COME HERE! YOU GOT TO SEE THIS. HURRY UP!"

Lamar ran to the door of his room, yelling for his father.

"Dad, you got to see this!" he said when his father entered the room. "YOU GOT TO!"

"What's going on? What's wrong?" Lamar's dad asked.

"Watch this," Lamar answered, and started the video. He moved to the beginning.

"What is this?" his father said.

"Just watch," Lamar told him.

After the shooting, the White man holding the gun looked at the Black man and then got into his car and remained there. Two sheriff's deputies drove up. One bent over the Black man on the ground. He stood up again and walked to the car where the other deputy stood talking to the White man who had fired the gun. Then he walked over to the blue car. After looking inside, he pulled a tire iron from the back seat and placed it on the ground next to the Black man. The second deputy moved quickly to the patrol car. It looked as if he was calling in a report.

"I'll be damned!" Lamar's father yelled. "Where did you get this?"

"I don't know, Dad. It was a link in an email someone sent. But I can't tell who sent it."

"This is what we've been looking for! This is the evidence that we need to show that Papa was murdered and there was a cover-up! You don't know who sent it?!"

"I really don't."

"There was no name or nothing?"

"No. I don't even recognize the email address. I don't know who sent it."

"Bring that laptop, Lamar. We have to take it to Attorney Smith. We have to show it to him. This video can change everything. I mean everything!"

"Shouldn't we let Mom and Kyra know?" Lamar asked as he and his father raced out of the room.

"You can phone them on the way to the motel and tell them to meet us there. I'm calling Mr. Smith now. Thank God. Thank God! Thank God!"

When Lamar and his father pulled into the driveway of the Morton Motel, they saw Ms. Phillips's car. She and Kyra had beaten them there.

"I can't wait to see this video," Lamar's mom greeted them. "I know this is God's hand at work."

"You don't know who sent it, Lamar?" Kyra asked.

"No, Kyra, I don't. I wish I knew."

"This is a miracle, I tell you!" Lamar's mom declared. "This is a miracle."

Attorney Smith greeted the Phillipses at the door. He had been staying at a motel room in Morton so he could be more accessible. The family hurried inside the room with Lamar clutching his laptop underneath his arm.

"What's the great news?" Attorney Smith inquired.

"We have something that just might be the answer to our prayers," Lamar's father told him. "Show the video to him, Lamar!"

Lamar placed his laptop on the desk near the bed.

"Hurry up and open it," Kyra insisted.

"I'm going as fast as I can, Kyra."

"He'll get there," their mother told her daughter. "Show some patience, Kyra."

"That boy is so slow," Kyra added, getting in the last word.

Lamar ignored her and started the video. When it began to play, they all moved in even closer. No one said a word until the gun was fired. When the video ended, Lamar's mom had already moved away, sobbing.

"That *was* Gramps," Kyra declared. "That was him, and Rutherford Thigpen just shot him. It was an execution!"

"Everyone's sure that was Mr. Phillips?" Mr. Smith questioned.

"That's him, all right," Lamar's father declared.

"And did you see what those deputies did? They went to Gramps's car, got that tire iron and placed it next to him." Kyra started pacing.

"This is big. Real big!" Mr. Smith told the Phillipses. "If this video is authentic, it will be like dropping a bomb in the middle of town. Not only is there murder, but there is a cover-up by those deputies. And all of it is on this video."

For a while, no one said a word.

"Gramps didn't do anything wrong!" Kyra said, finally breaking the silence. "They just lied on him!"

"Lamar, are you sure you don't know who sent the email?" Attorney Smith asked.

"No, Mr. Smith. I don't. There's no name in the email. I don't recognize the email address."

Lamar's mom turned away as she wiped the tears from her eyes.

"Why was it sent to you?" she asked her son. "Why would someone send it to you?"

"I don't know, Mom," Lamar answered. "I don't have any idea."

"Whoever sent it had to be there when it happened. They had to have witnessed the whole thing."

"Maybe so, Ms. Phillips," Attorney Smith said. Now he was pacing like Kyra.

"Or maybe someone gave the video to whoever sent it," he suggested. "We have to get this video to someone we can trust," he said, turning to Lamar. "If we take it to the prosecutor, or even to the police here in Morton, there is no telling what they will do with it, or what they will say about it. We need someone on our side. Or, at best, someone who is neutral. If there's someone in the media we can trust, they can probably help find out who sent the video and let us know whether it's authentic."

"What about Drayton Wilkerson, the reporter for WKCU News 6?" Lamar offered. "He's been covering the protests and everything. I've talked to him a few times. He gave me his business card."

"I think his coverage has been fair, considering it's here in this state," Kyra interjected. Coming from her, that was an endorsement.

"Yes, he has been fair," Lamar's dad added.

"Let's give Wilkerson a call," Attorney Smith said.

Lamar pulled the business card from his back pocket and dialed the number on the card.

"Hello," a voice answered.

"Mr. Wilkerson, this is Lamar Phillips. You know, the kid from Morton with the video camcorder. We got something important—"

Before Lamar could finish, Mr. Smith had taken the phone from him.

"Mr. Wilkerson, I'm Attorney Henry L. Smith. I think we've seen each other a few times during the last week. As you know, I represent the Phillips family. Listen, we have something extremely important to share, and we want to give you the scoop on it. I can't tell you over the phone. But I can assure you it could be a bombshell. . . . When will you come to Morton again. . . . You're already here? . . . We're at the Morton Motel, room 312. . . . All right. See you soon."

After ending the call, Mr. Smith gave the cell phone back to Lamar. "I'm sorry, Lamar. But I wanted to make sure Wilkerson understood what we have here. He's arriving in ten minutes."

When there was a knock at the door, everyone knew it was Drayton Wilkerson and Victor. Drayton nodded to everyone, but Lamar received a smile from him. Lamar smiled back.

"Come in," Attorney Smith welcomed him. "Thank you for coming. We have something to show you that I think you'll find *very, very* interesting. Lamar, can you please show him what we have?"

Lamar played the video for Drayton, who couldn't believe what he had just seen.

"Where did you get this?!" he asked, his mouth open.

"Someone sent it to Lamar," Mr. Smith told him. "Anonymously."

"Has it been verified?"

"That's why we called you. You can help determine that. We believe it is authentic and that it shows what really happened between Mr. Phillips and Mr. Thigpen."

Drayton turned to Lamar. "You don't have an idea who sent it, Lamar?"

"No! No!"

"Perhaps you can look into it, Mr. Wilkerson," Attorney Smith told the reporter. "If it's authentic, will your station run it? We would rather make it public that way before turning it over to the authorities."

"You don't trust them?" Drayton asked.

"No, Mr. Wilkerson, we don't. Would you if you were us?"

Drayton Wilkerson hesitated for a long moment, pondering the question. He looked at Victor, who just shrugged, then turned to Mr. Smith again.

"I understand," he answered. "I understand. Lamar, can you forward the email to me? My email address is on the back of the card I gave you. You still have it?"

"Yeah," Lamar answered. He quickly forwarded the email to Drayton.

"I thank you all for your trust," he told the Phillipses and Attorney Smith. "I'm humbled by your faith in me. I assure you I will get on this. Like you, I think this is an authentic video, too. And that means someone out there witnessed the incident. I hope to have news for you soon."

Drayton smiled at Lamar again. "I think I have you to thank for this scoop, Lamar."

Lamar smiled back.

"I've been checking him out," Drayton told the others. "He's ready."

"But I ain't a professional like you guys."

"You will get there. Believe me, you will get there."

Drayton and Victor left the room, closing the door behind them. Lamar's mother moved to the motel window and watched them walk back to their car.

"I told y'all we have to have faith," she said. "You have to have faith!"

"We must keep this video to ourselves for now," Attorney Smith warned everyone. "We must be sure that everything lines up. So, let's wait until we hear back from Drayton. We can't afford a misstep. I'm hoping that with the staff and resources the station has, they'll be able to find out who sent the video."

"Whoever sent it must be scared to death," Lamar's father said. "They must know what making this video public will do."

"And if they sent it, that means they must have a conscience," Lamar's mom added.

CHAPTER 20

"I wonder if it's coming on first," Kyra said to no one in particular.

"I would think so," her father said. "It's a big deal! Can't be anything bigger than this."

Following another day of protest, the Phillips family sat in their living room, anxiously watching for the ten p.m. news to start. Drayton Wilkerson had kept his word. The video would be shown as a breaking news story.

"I'm nervous," Lamar's father admitted.

"You're not alone," his wife replied. "I think we all are, but it's a good nervousness."

Suddenly, the news theme began.

"This is WKCU News 6 at ten with Andrea Alleman, Grant Bloomberg with the weather and Chad Foxworth with sports," the announcer said above the blaring music.

"Good evening," Andrea Alleman welcomed the viewers. "The mayor makes an important decision, a local college receives a major grant, death on the river—these are three of our leading stories tonight. But first, we have a WKCU News 6 exclusive on the ongoing story out of Morton. With more, we turn to Drayton Wilkerson, who has followed the story from the beginning. Drayton."

"Thank you, Andrea. As you know, we have been covering the killing of Joshua Phillips, the elderly Black man who was shot and killed by Rutherford Thigpen just outside of Morton a few weeks ago. Authorities have not pressed charges in the case because Mr. Thigpen has claimed self-defense and because no witness to the incident has emerged. Well, WKCU News 6 has unearthed a video of the incident that will certainly change everything about this case. The video was sent anonymously to the family of Mr. Joshua Phillips. The family called this reporter yesterday to submit the video to WKCU News 6. After hours of careful examination by our staff and by outside experts, we have determined that the video is authentic. We are still trying to determine who sent it. And we will continue to investigate. I warn you that the video is quite graphic. So, parents, you may want to move young children away from the screen while it plays."

After the video ended, Drayton spoke again. "As you can see, Mr. Phillips appears to be unarmed when he is shot. The two sheriff's deputies who investigated the incident appear to be involved in a cover-up. One of them gets a tire iron from Mr. Phillips's car and places it near his body. There are so many questions that need answers. We will keep you informed as this story continues to unfold. Back to you, Andrea."

"Drayton, what a development! Congratulations to you for uncovering the truth."

"Andrea, I must thank the Phillips family for reaching out to me and trusting me to report it. We have a call out to the DA's office in Morton and are waiting to get their response. We'll certainly stay on top of this."

"Thank you, Drayton. That's some reporting."

"I'm just doing my job, Andrea. Just doing my job."

Kyra lowered the volume on the television just as her father's cell phone rang.

"Drayton did an excellent job, don't you think?" Attorney Smith asked Lamar's father on the other end.

"He certainly did," Lamar's father answered.

"I'm going to set up an appointment with the district attorney for tomorrow morning," Attorney Smith advised. "I want you all to meet me at his office. I know they are aware of the video. I want to see what they have to say now. I'd like Kyra and Lamar to go, too. I think it's more impactful to show up as a family. Can the children skip school?"

"School won't be a problem. We'll be there. Oh, and thank you. I think things are starting to turn around."

"Get a good night's sleep. All of you. You need it."

"We will. You have a good night."

CHAPTER 21

"You ready?" Lamar's mother asked, already dressed in her favorite blue pantsuit.

"I'm ready, Mom."

"You better grab a bowl of cereal before we leave. I don't want you to go on an empty stomach."

Lamar ran into Kyra, who was dressed in a long white skirt and matching white top, on the way to get his breakfast.

"If Philyaw could see you now," he joked.

"Get out of here, boy! You want a smackdown?"

Soon the Phillipses settled into the car. A neighbor shouted to them as it pulled out of the driveway.

"I'm sho' glad y'all got that video!"

"So are we, Geraldine," Lamar's mom answered. The

neighbor waved as the car moved down dusty Jones Street.

Attorney Smith had already arrived at the DA's office and waited at the entrance.

"Are you ready?" he asked them.

"As ready as we'll ever be," Lamar's father answered. Lamar held his laptop tightly as they entered the building.

A middle-aged White woman greeted them. Looking up from the desk, she asked, "What can I do for y'all?"

"We're here to see District Attorney Caulfield," Mr. Smith told her. "We have an appointment."

Lamar looked around the room. Nicely framed photos of former district attorneys adorned the walls. None were Black, and none were female. The receptionist directed them to a large room where a thin, middle-aged White man sat behind a large mahogany desk. He examined Mr. Smith and the Phillipses closely.

"Come in. Come in," he told them, finally acknowledging their presence. "I'm just finishing something here."

He stood and extended a hand to Attorney Smith.

"You're Attorney Smith? You look just like you do on television."

"Yes, I am," Attorney Smith responded, and then turned to the Phillips family. "I'm sure you know the

Phillipses, too. This is Mr. and Ms. Phillips, their daughter, Kyra, and son, Lamar."

"Glad to meet y'all. Now, what's this I hear about a video? Why didn't y'all bring it to us?"

"Well, Mr. Caulfield, we thought our best move was to give it to someone we knew at the television station," Attorney Smith answered.

"I see. So, y'all don't trust the district attorney's office? Is that what I'm hearing?"

No one answered. Mr. Caulfield moved on.

"Okay. Now how did y'all come by this video? Neither the sheriff's office nor the Morton Police Department have been able to turn up anything."

"As the news reporter said, someone emailed it to Lamar," Attorney Smith answered. "Anonymously. Will you explain it, Lamar?"

"Uh . . . uh . . . I just checked my email messages and there it was," Lamar told the DA, nervous that the spotlight was on him. "At first, I thought it was someone trying to scam me. But when I clicked on the link, there was the video. That's about it."

"I'm sure you won't mind if the family sits down, would you, Mr. Caulfield?"

"Not at all, Mr. Smith. Not at all. Y'all make yourselves comfortable."

Lamar's mom and dad sat, but Kyra and Lamar didn't. Neither did Attorney Smith. Kyra stood erect, her eyes fastened on the district attorney.

"So, Lawrence, you don't—"

"His name isn't Lawrence," Kyra corrected the DA quickly. "His name is Lamar."

"Sorry about that." The DA apologized after staring at Kyra for a long moment.

"So, Lamar, you don't have any idea who sent you the video?" he continued.

"No, I don't. WKCU News 6 says they are trying to find out who emailed it," Lamar answered.

"You don't mind if we keep your laptop for a few days, do you?" the DA asked Lamar politely.

"No, he doesn't mind," Attorney Smith answered for Lamar. "If we said no, you would issue a subpoena for it anyway," he added.

"I am happy we won't have to do that, Mr. Smith," the DA said, moving a stack of papers on his desk to make room for Lamar's laptop.

"All right. Let's take a look at it. You can put your laptop right here. There's an outlet underneath if you need to plug it in."

"It's fully charged," Lamar told him.

Lamar placed the laptop on the desk and went quickly

to the email message and clicked on the link. Mr. Caulfield stood behind him. Once the video started, Lamar moved away so the district attorney could get a closer look. Mr. Caulfield didn't say a word. But his face tightened, and his body tensed. Lamar glanced at Kyra to get her reaction. When he was unsure how to respond to something, she was his barometer. When the video reached the section where the tire iron was removed from Joshua Phillips's car, Mr. Caulfield's face got even tighter.

"You sure you don't know who sent this?" he asked Lamar curtly again, turning away from the laptop.

"No!" Lamar replied.

Mr. Caulfield reached for the phone on his desk.

"Excuse me," he told his visitors before speaking into the receiver. "Mrs. Tyler, tell Jim to come in here," he told his secretary.

What is the DA up to? Lamar wondered. They all knew he had seen the video when it aired on the news last night. He probably had already recorded a copy of it.

A younger man, perhaps in his thirties, entered the office. The DA said, "This is James Westerfield. Jim handles all of our public relations around here. Jim, this is the Phillips family, relatives of the late Mr. Joshua Phillips, and their attorney, Mr. Smith." Jim nodded. The Phillipses and Attorney Smith remained silent.

"Jim, we wanna set up a press conference with the Phillipses and their attorney around eleven this morning. We want to let the public know that we're on top of this case. Can you get the press here by eleven?"

"No problem," Jim said. "Consider it done."

"Wait! Wait!" Kyra interrupted. "What's this press conference about? Are you *telling* us to be there, or are you *asking* us?"

The district attorney and his public relations man were both caught off guard by Kyra's boldness.

"Well, I'm requesting that you join us," the DA answered. "You see, this town is a powder keg. We should do anything we can to keep it from being ignited."

"Mr. Caulfield, it's a little late, isn't it?" Attorney Smith spoke up, walking closer to the DA. "There is no need for us to attend this press conference. We plan to address our group later today. The cat's out of the bag now, and we will get justice for Mr. Phillips. I hope you are preparing arrest warrants, at least three of them."

Lamar watched Attorney Smith closely. *He's tough,* Lamar thought. *If I wasn't gonna be a filmmaker, maybe I'd be a lawyer just like him.* Then Lamar looked at the DA for his reaction.

"We will do our job, sir!" the DA snapped. Attorney Smith's defiant tone had agitated the veteran district attorney. Now he looked at Attorney Smith as if he were a worthy adversary. Clearly, Attorney Smith was under-mining his authority. He gathered himself and repeated, "As I said earlier, we will do our job, sir!"

DA Caulfield turned to his public relations man.

"I'll talk to you later, Jim," he told him.

"Yes, sir," Jim answered. After staring at the Phillipses and their lawyer, he left.

"What I plan to do," the DA addressed Attorney Smith again, "is announce that our office and the sheriff's de-partment are investigating this video and that we're using all of our resources to find out just what happened. I hope we have your support as we move forward with this."

"You'll always have our support to do the right thing," Attorney Smith offered.

After they left the DA's office, the attorney told the family, "He wanted to use us. Kyra saw through it right away. The DA never said anything about making an ar-rest. I bet they're trying to find a way to delegitimize the video. In a small town like this, cronyism is a big deal. We have to be very cautious. We still have work to do. Let's grab an early lunch. By the time we finish, today's pro-test will have started. We have to let *our* supporters know what's happening."

"I sure hope they don't mess up my laptop," Lamar mused. "I got a lot saved on it."

CHAPTER 22

Lamar was happy he didn't have to go to school after the meeting with the DA. While his parents, Kyra and Attorney Smith joined the protestors, Lamar sat on the courthouse steps. As he checked out his camcorder, his cell phone rang.

"Lamar, this is Jeff!"

Lamar was stunned.

"Jeff?"

"Yeah, it's me. Where are you?" Jeff asked.

"I'm at the protest. What's up? What happened to you? Why you stopped coming to Morton?" Lamar was full of questions.

"I'm on the corner of Oak and Houston Streets," Jeff said, sounding nervous. "I need to see you."

"Now?!"

"Yeah, now. It's important, Lamar. Really important."

"I'm on the way."

Lamar pushed the cell phone back into his pocket and rushed off.

When he neared the corner of Oak and Houston Streets, he saw Jeff pacing. Seeing him reminded Lamar how much he had missed the talks they used to have. No one else in Morton had the interest in filmmaking that Jeff had. He was the only one in Morton who really understood the creative side of Lamar. And Lamar was the only one who understood that side of Jeff.

Lamar thought about the movie he and Jeff had planned to work on. He had been so excited about it. But now it looked as if it wouldn't happen.

"What's up, bro?" Lamar asked when he reached the corner.

"You, bro!"

Lamar smiled at Jeff's reply.

"Been a while, dude," he told Jeff playfully.

"Yeah, a while."

Lamar could tell Jeff was uncomfortable. He wouldn't even look Lamar in the eye. Jeff checked every car that passed by, too, as if he was expecting someone to drive up.

"Where have you been?" Lamar asked Jeff.

"Around," said Jeff. "I'm going to another school now. My parents made me."

"You finished your synopsis for that movie we planned to do?" Lamar asked.

"Naw," Jeff answered. "You?"

"Too much happening. I can't focus on it," Lamar answered.

"Yeah. A lot happening with me, too. I really wanted to do it."

"Me too. So what's the deal?" Lamar asked pointedly. "Why you wanna see me?"

Finally, Jeff looked at his old friend.

"I sent that video," he told him.

"What?! You sent it!!" Lamar almost dropped his video camcorder.

"Yeah, I sent it. I couldn't think of any other way to get it to you. I couldn't drop it off at your house, now, could I?"

"Wow! What can I say, Jeff? I never thought it was you. When you stopped coming to Morton, I didn't think I'd ever see you again."

"I didn't know you were gonna give the video to the television station," Jeff complained. He started pacing the sidewalk again. Now Lamar was panicking. Was Jeff in trouble?

"The people at the television station are gonna find

out I sent the video!" Jeff said, tearing up. "When they do, they're gonna make my name public, and my father's, too."

Lamar felt sorry for Jeff. He understood the predicament he faced. But what else could he and his family do? They couldn't just sit on the video and let his grandfather's murderer go free. So many people had heard the lies that were told about his Gramps. He deserved justice.

"Jeff, I'm sorry," he told his friend. "Our lawyer suggested that we make the video public. We had to get the video out there. We had to!"

Jeff took in a big breath of air and exhaled it long and slow.

"I know. I know," he said.

Lamar grabbed Jeff's hand and held it firmly.

"Jeff, did you record the video?" he asked his friend. "Were you there when it all happened? You couldn't have been there. You went to school that day."

Jeff inhaled again, but the air he released this time rushed out.

"It was my father. He recorded it on his cell phone."

"Your *father*?"

An approaching car made Jeff stop. He turned away from Lamar and walked a few steps up the sidewalk as if he and Lamar were not together. After the car passed, he walked back to where Lamar was standing.

"You scared, Jeff?"

"Yeah, I'm scared! My father, too."

"Jeff, why did your father record what happened?"

It didn't make sense to Lamar. He knew that Jeff's father hadn't wanted Jeff and Lamar to be friends. And Jeff had hinted that his father didn't like Black people. So, why would his father videotape an incident that would clear a Black man and indict a White man?

"He was on his way to work when he saw the accident," Jeff explained. "He stopped and pulled to the side of the road and started recording with his cell phone. He didn't know what was going to happen. He was just recording. If he knew, he probably wouldn't have done it."

"He could have erased it."

"That's what he was going to do after he showed it to us, especially when Mr. Thigpen told everyone your grandfather had tried to attack him. Lamar, my father and Mr. Thigpen's son played on the same high school football team. My daddy wasn't gonna let anybody see that video. So I sneaked his cell phone and forwarded the video to my phone. Then I sent it to you. I just didn't think it was right for your grandfather to be killed like that. For no reason at all. Now my father's scared to death. I thought he was gonna kill me when he found out I had sent the video."

"That was a brave thing to do, Jeff."

"Brave? Yeah, right. I'm scared to death, too."

"So, what're you gonna do? Your father gonna talk to the police?"

"No. No way. We're leaving town, Lamar."

"Leaving town?"

"Yeah. Dad and Mom are at the house packing now. We're going to Dallas to stay with my uncle for a while. Dad knows they will eventually try to force him to point the finger at Mr. Thigpen. And he don't wanna do that."

"But he has to, Jeff! It's the truth."

"It ain't that simple, Lamar. Do you know what would happen even if my father could overcome his prejudice and tell the truth about what happened? He'd be shunned by his friends. They'd kick him out of the Masons. He wouldn't be able to go hunting with his buddies. He wouldn't be able to play golf at the course anymore. My father's life would be over. And all because of me!"

The two friends stared at each other silently. Neither knew what to say. They were both forced to navigate through a world they hadn't created. But they still had to find their own way in it.

"It's messed up, ain't it, Lamar?"

"Yeah, it is, Jeff."

"Remember when you told me you were gonna do a

documentary about your grandfather?" Jeff asked, looking away.

"When we were in the media center at school? That's what you talkin' 'bout?"

"Yeah."

"I remember," Lamar replied.

"Remember that I got a little upset?"

"I thought you were acting kinda funny."

"Well, I know about the time your grandfather led that protest in town. My relatives still talk about it. To them, that was the time everything changed for the worse in Morton. That was when the Colored started to take over. But they didn't say Colored. I wanna get away from all that. You know what I mean. See, Lamar, my grandfather, the one who wanted to be an actor and taught me about the ol' movies. He wasn't like that. He had traveled and seen a lot. He didn't think like they did. He used to get into arguments with them all the time, especially with my dad. That's why my grandfather left. But I hope you're gonna make that documentary about your grandfather. I really do."

Lamar didn't know how to respond to Jeff sharing so much with him. He wished he could help him. He knew Jeff was his friend, because why else would he do something that could get him and his father in trouble?

Why else would he oppose his father's view of the world and the views of the people he had to be around every day? Lamar thought about the movies he and Jeff used to talk about . . . the ones from the golden age, with Bogey, Spencer Tracy and all the others that Jeff liked so much. Lamar remembered the movie project they had planned to do before Gramps was killed. Now, Jeff was leaving town and he might never return to Morton. If he and his family did return, it wouldn't be the same for them. Jeff probably wouldn't be attending Morton Middle School again.

"We'll be leaving tomorrow morning." Jeff spoke up, breaking the silence. "They'll probably find out that the video came from my cell phone. They can find out anything. Then they'll find out my father recorded it. That reporter from WKCU News 6 will keep asking questions. My father says if he's not here, they can't bother him. Even if they find him, he says he ain't gonna say anything."

Another car approached. Jeff jumped.

"I've gotta get back. Nobody knows I'm here. Dad would kill me if he knew. I'm gonna walk down to Grove Street to catch the bus. I guess I'll see you later."

"Yeah. See you later, Jeff."

Lamar extended his right hand in a fist and Jeff knew just what to do. He made a fist, too, and the two friends fist-bumped. But this time a fist bump wasn't sufficient. So they hugged, and when they pulled away, they fist-bumped again.

Lamar watched as Jeff jogged down the sidewalk. He wondered if this was the last time he would see his friend.

CHAPTER 23

"I've got some news," Lamar yelled out just before reaching his dad and mom, Kyra, Attorney Smith and Reverend Thurmond.

"I hope it's worth interrupting us," Kyra warned.

"You bet it is," Lamar confirmed. "I know who emailed the video."

That caught everyone's attention. All eyes fell on Lamar.

"It was Jeff."

"Jeff? You mean that little White boy you always talking to about movies?" Kyra questioned.

"Don't rag on him, Kyra." Lamar felt himself getting angry. He knew what his friend was going through. "He's a good dude. He's my friend."

"How did you find out, Lamar?" Attorney Smith asked.

"Jeff told me. I just talked with him. He emailed the video, but he didn't record it. His father did. But I don't want to get Jeff in trouble."

"His father?" they all said at the same time.

"Yeah. He was on his way to work that morning when he saw the accident. He parked his car and started recording the whole thing with his cell phone."

"Nobody else knows?" Attorney Smith asked.

"I don't think so. Jeff took it from his father's cell phone and emailed it to me. He said his father is scared. They're gonna leave in the morning to go to Dallas, where Jeff's uncle lives."

"We'd better get to the district attorney with this," Attorney Smith asserted. "Jeff's father can be compelled to testify."

"Mr. Smith, I feel kinda bad," Lamar lamented. "Jeff is my friend. I don't wanna get him in trouble."

"Lamar, there is no other choice. If we don't take this to the district attorney, the man who murdered your grandfather could go free."

"Lamar, son, all you're doing is telling the truth," Reverend Thurmond added. "I feel for your friend. But he must know that you have no choice but to report it. That's probably why he told you."

The walk to the district attorney's office seemed to take forever. Lamar kept thinking about Jeff. *What will happen to him? What will his father do to him? Will he have to move away forever?*

When they entered the district attorney's office, the receptionist escorted them inside. Mr. Caulfield was seated behind his desk as before. He didn't say a word but just looked up.

"Mr. Caulfield," Mr. Smith said directly and quickly, "we know who recorded the video."

The DA rose from his desk, a flustered look on his face.

"Which means that person saw *everything* that happened," Mr. Smith added.

Does the DA really want to know? Lamar wondered. *This means he will have to do something about Gramps's murder. There is no way around the video now that there's an eyewitness.*

"Who is it?" the DA asked.

"It's the father of someone Lamar knows," Attorney Smith answered. "Tell Mr. Caulfield who it is, Lamar."

"Mr. Wilson. My friend's father's name is Mr. Craig Wilson."

"Craig Wilson? Craig Wilson." Mr. Caulfield repeated the name twice.

"Do you know him, Mr. Caulfield?" Attorney Smith asked.

"Yes. He's not a friend, but I know who he is. Are you sure about this, Lawr—I mean, Lamar?"

"He's sure, Mr. Caulfield," Attorney Smith answered instead. "I assume arrests will be made after you've had a chance to talk with Mr. Wilson. I think we're past the questioning stage."

"I appreciate your concern," DA Caulfield said caustically to Attorney Smith. "But you are *not* the district attorney of this parish. I am. We will handle this case the way we see fit. Now, I thank you for bringing me this information. But we will not be pushed or forced into taking any actions if we don't think they're warranted."

"We just want you to do what's right. What's fair and just. We want you to follow the law."

"We will follow the case where the evidence leads us, Mr. Smith."

"The eyes of the nation and the world are on you, Mr. Caulfield. People are demanding justice."

Mr. Caulfield moved away from his desk.

"Mr. Smith, I have been the district attorney of this parish for fifteen years. I don't need anybody to tell me how to do my job. Especially you. You don't even live in this town or this parish. Thomasville is not in Jackson Parish. You are an outsider, sir. So don't lecture me."

"Wait, Mr. Caulfield. Attorney Smith represents this family," Reverend Thurmond intervened. "And I'm the family's pastor. We speak with one voice. All we're trying to do here is make sure there is justice. A man has been killed. If it wasn't a Black man who was killed by a White man, there would be no problem. Justice would be served."

"Is that your way of calling me a racist, Reverend? Are you saying that if it had been a White person who was killed, I would do things differently? Is that what you're saying? I'll have you know that I have been fairer to Black people than any other district attorney in the history of this parish. I was the first to hire a Black person on my staff. I supported Mayor Johnson in his bid for reelection. I dare you to imply that I am a racist."

"Mr. Caulfield, we came here to give you some important information about the case. We didn't come to upset you or to get into a fight with you," Attorney Smith said.

"Mr. Smith, the reverend has implied that I am a racist. Do you think I should sit still for that?"

"I don't think he called you a racist, Mr. Caulfield. But if that's the way you heard it, there isn't anything we can do about that. We have to get back to our supporters so we can make them aware of this new development. We wanted to give the information to your office first. We have done that."

Mr. Caulfield returned to his chair. He shuffled some papers around, then looked up at Attorney Smith.

"I thank you, Attorney Smith, for letting me know. Excuse me. We have work to do."

Attorney Smith nodded and opened the door for the Phillips family and Reverend Thurmond to leave the office. On the way back to the protest, Lamar caught up with Attorney Smith.

"Do we have to let everyone know that it was Jeff's father who recorded the video? I feel so bad for Jeff. I wish there was another way. Jeff's my friend."

"There isn't, Lamar. Unfortunately, securing justice is very often messy, and sometimes innocent people get hurt. Sometimes the truth hurts. Do you understand?"

"Yeah, I guess so," Lamar answered. "I guess so."

CHAPTER 24

"Hey, Lamar. Are you going to the DA's press conference?" Drayton Wilkerson asked as he and Victor walked past the stage where Lamar was standing with his video camcorder. "We're going over now to cover it. I think he has an announcement about the video. You're not going? This could be big news."

"Where is the press conference?" Lamar asked Drayton.

"In front of his building," Drayton answered as he and Victor hurried off.

Lamar quickly shared the information with his parents, Kyra, Attorney Smith and Reverend Thurmond.

"We just left his office a little while ago," Lamar's father said.

"We better get over there to see what's going on," Attorney Smith suggested.

When they arrived, Mr. Caulfield had already begun the press conference. Standing next to him were Jim Westerfield, his public relations man, and other people Lamar didn't know. Newspaper and other TV reporters were there, too. Drayton Wilkerson, standing near the front, waved when he spotted Lamar. Lamar waved back.

"Good afternoon. For those of you who don't know me, I'm John Caulfield, district attorney for this parish. With me are my assistant, Ike Kendricks; Jim Westerfield, from our public information department; Peter Conforte, the sheriff of this parish; and James Weston, president of the police jury. For those of you who are not from the state, and I see there are a few of you, the police jury is the legislative governing body for the parish.

"We called this press conference to provide an update on the case you all have been following lately. As you may know, a video recording was aired on WKCU News 6. Supposedly, it captures the interaction between Mr. Joshua Phillips, the victim, and Mr. Rutherford Thigpen, who fired the shots that killed Mr. Phillips. Also shown on the video are sheriff's deputies, whose actions following the incident are in question. Our department, as well as the sheriff's department and the Morton Police Department, are undertaking a thorough investigation to determine the authenticity of the recording. As you may know, WKCU News 6 did not disclose the name of the person who sent the video."

"Have any arrests been made?" Drayton Wilkerson yelled out, interrupting the DA.

"I will get to that, sir. Please, show a little patience. Just recently," continued Mr. Caulfield, "we were given information that will, perhaps, not only identify who sent the video but who recorded it."

"That means there is an eyewitness?" another news reporter questioned the stern-faced DA.

"What I can say," he responded, "is all the information we have received is being investigated thoroughly. Now, regarding the question about arrests. No, no one has been arrested. But people are being questioned as we speak."

"Mr. Caulfield, don't you have enough evidence to make an arrest?" Drayton continued to probe. "The video is quite revealing, sir."

"Caulfield is just a lot of talk," Kyra whispered to Lamar. "He's just trying to get ahead of this so he can put his spin on it."

"As I said earlier," the determined DA replied, "we are doing a thorough investigation. We're working on our schedule and not anyone else's. We resent anyone implying that this office will not handle this case fairly. We will go where the evidence leads us. Again, the purpose of this news conference is to provide an update as more information comes in. We will schedule another news conference tomorrow. We'll let you know the time. Now, we have to get back to work."

Reporters scrambled to throw more questions at the district attorney. But their efforts were in vain.

"See you tomorrow," the DA said, waving to them as he and his group hurriedly walked back into the building.

CHAPTER 25

Lamar sat on the steps of the post office build-ing, taking a much-needed rest. It had been a full day. There were the meetings with the district attorney, the one with Jeff, the press conference. So much had happened that he hadn't missed T.C., who had gone with his family to visit his ailing grandmother. When he looked up, he saw his friend approaching.

"I didn't think I would be able to get here before the protest ended," he told Lamar.

"How's your grandmother?" Lamar asked.

"She's okay. Why didn't you answer my call?"

"Oh, wow. I forgot to turn my phone back on. I turned it off during all those meetings."

When he checked, there was a message. *"Lamar. This is Jeff. Call me back."*

Lamar knew it had to be important. He could hear how frantic Jeff sounded.

He returned the call quickly. "Jeff? This is Lamar. What's up?"

"I tried to reach you," Jeff said.

"Yeah, I had turned off my phone."

"Tell Jeff I said hello," T.C. interrupted. "Tell him I miss his ugly face."

Lamar ignored T.C.

"What's up, Jeff?"

"He did it, Lamar!" an excited Jeff told Lamar. "My dad did it!"

"Did what, Jeff? What're you talking about?"

"He told what he saw! He didn't want to, but he did. Two investigators came by the house. They took a statement from him. And he told the truth. He told them everything that he saw."

"I don't believe it!"

"I didn't believe it either, Lamar," Jeff exclaimed. "But he did it!"

"What happened?" T.C. asked, anxious to know what all the excitement was about. Again, Lamar ignored him.

"Jeff, that's great news."

"What's great news? What are y'all talking about?" T.C. was beside himself with curiosity.

"Jeff's father told the police what he saw when Gramps was killed," Lamar finally told him.

"YES!" T.C. responded, thrusting a fist into the air.

"So you won't have to leave now, will you, Jeff?"

"Are you kidding, Lamar?! We *really* have to leave now. Dad don't want to face his friends. So we're still going to Dallas. But he said he'll come back for the trial. Maybe things will cool down after a while. Maybe."

"I sure wish you didn't have to leave. We didn't get to do that film together."

"No, we didn't. Maybe later, huh?"

"When *are* you leaving?"

"This evening. We're all packed. We would have been gone already if the investigators hadn't come by. They didn't seem like they wanted Dad to talk. But he did. He surprised me."

"Maybe it was because of you, Jeff."

"You think?"

"I wouldn't doubt it at all."

"Yeah. Well, I've got to go. Dallas is about a four-hour drive. At least I'll finally be in a big town where there is a lot to do."

As he held the cell phone to his ear, Lamar thought about the new things he had learned from Jeff and that Jeff had learned from him. *If Jeff was Black or if I was*

White, Jeff would be my running buddy just like T.C., Lamar thought.

"Jeff," Lamar said to his friend, "no matter what happens, let's stay in touch. Let's check in with each other. Actually, I hope you come back to Morton Middle School."

"Me too," Jeff replied. "I like Morton. You know, Lamar, your grandfather was right to stand up and fight to change things back in the Civil Rights Movement days. That's what we gotta do. Well, I gotta go. But I'll call you when I get to Dallas. I'm gonna start working on that synopsis again. And I'll let you know how it's going."

"Me too," Lamar responded.

"Later, Lamar," Jeff said.

"Yeah, Jeff. Later. Make sure you call me, now."

"You got it."

Lamar ended the call.

"You ain't crying, are you, Lamar?" T.C. asked.

"No, I ain't crying," Lamar answered, trying to brush off T.C.'s inquiry. He turned away so T.C. couldn't see the tears that had begun to well up in his eyes.

CHAPTER 26

"**Lamar. The DA called another press confer-**ence for five thirty," Drayton said as he ran past Lamar and T.C., who were still sitting on the steps of the post office. Victor followed him, holding tightly to his camera. "I think it's something big," Drayton added.

Lamar thought about going to get his family. But it was almost 5:30. So he and T.C. ran behind Drayton and Victor.

They arrived just in time to see DA Caulfield tap on the microphone. The DA had more people with him this time. Mayor Johnson was there. Jim Westerfield, the DA's PR man. Members of the Morton town council. Morton's chief of police. Lamar saw his family, Attorney Smith and Reverend Thurmond approaching from a distance.

"I think we have to stop meeting like this," the DA

said. But his joke fell flat. So he continued with the real purpose of the press conference. "You have probably heard that a major break has occurred in the Joshua Phillips case. That's why we have called a second press conference.

"As I told you all during the first press conference, we are going to conduct a thorough investigation. And we are going to follow where the evidence leads. We are not going to yield to pressure from anyone. But we are going to let our legal system do its work. For those of you who thought justice wouldn't prevail, you're wrong."

"Mr. Caulfield, you called us here because there is new evidence in the case?" one of the reporters asked impatiently. "Is that true?"

"Yes, sir, that is true. We have interviewed and gotten a statement from an eyewitness to the incident that occurred on Highway 76. Based on his statement, the sheriff's department has placed deputies Gregory Nelson and Andrew Thornton on unpaid leave while the department conducts a thorough investigation. What we saw on the video was disturbing and is not representative of the fine men and women who serve in the sheriff's department. Finally, a warrant for the arrest of Mr. Rutherford Thigpen has already been issued."

"What will Mr. Thigpen be charged with?" asked a reporter.

"That will be determined," the DA answered.

"Will the two sheriff's deputies be charged?" a second reporter inquired.

"We are investigating their involvement."

"From the video, it looks as if Mr. Thigpen shot Mr. Phillips without cause. And it looks as if the sheriff's deputies covered it up. Am I right about that, sir?" yet another reporter asked.

"As I said, we'll be looking into everything," Mr. Caulfield replied, agitated. "But as I told you, those two deputies are on unpaid leave pending further investigation."

"Mr. Caulfield, isn't it true, sir, that the family of the victim has done the real investigative work in this case?" Drayton asked, joining the chorus of questioners. "If not for them, this case would have been dropped. Is that a true statement?"

"I resent those accusations!" Mr. Caulfield roared back. "Yes, it's true that the Phillips family has been helpful to us. But we have been focused on this case from the beginning. And we continue to do so!"

Another reporter made her way up front. "Mr. Caulfield, we have been doing research into past cases in this parish where Black citizens have been shot, some killed, by White citizens. The vast majority of those cases never went to trial, or the perpetrators received extremely light sentences. Will it be like that in this case? If not, can you tell us why it won't be?"

"Listen, I am not here to discuss past cases! The purpose of this press conference is to provide an update on this particular case. We're still in the early stages of this investigation, and we will continue to provide updates. We have much yet to do."

"What kind of charges are you considering, Mr. Caulfield?" Drayton asked as the DA turned to leave.

Jim Westerfield stepped up to the mic. "No more questions," he announced. "We'll let you know when the next press conference will be scheduled. Thank you all for coming."

By the time the announcement ended, the DA and his entourage had made their way into the building. The reporters followed, peppering them with questions to which they didn't respond.

"They're still trying to find a way out of this," Attorney Smith told the Phillips family and Reverend Thurmond.

"They can't get around it, can they?" Lamar's father asked.

"It will be difficult," answered Attorney Smith. "We've got to keep the pressure on."

CHAPTER 27

Later that evening, Lamar yelled from the living room. "There's breaking news! I think they arrested Mr. Thigpen."

Kyra, Lamar's parents and Attorney Smith rushed in. Drayton flashed onto the television screen.

"This is Drayton Wilkerson from WKCU News 6 reporting from in front of the courthouse in Morton, Louisiana. We are waiting for sheriff's deputies to arrive. We understand Rutherford Thigpen, the man who shot and killed Joshua Phillips weeks ago, has been placed under arrest at his home and is being brought here for booking. You may remember that, initially, Mr. Thigpen said he shot Mr. Phillips in self-defense. A cell phone recording that this station aired seems to show that it wasn't self-defense. As a result, a warrant was issued for Mr. Thigpen's arrest."

Lamar leaped into the air. Kyra clapped her hands enthusiastically. Their parents embraced. Even a normally cool Attorney Smith couldn't contain his excitement.

"Wait. Wait. Let's hear the rest of it," Kyra said, turning up the volume.

"The man who recorded the video, Mr. Craig Wilson, has already been interviewed. Black people in Morton, and some White supporters, who have been protesting for nearly a week to get justice in the case, have been calling for the arrest of Mr. Thigpen. They feel the shooting was racially motivated. A former businessman in Morton, Mr. Thigpen once served on the Morton town council. He once headed the local chapter of the Ku Klux Klan. I think the sheriff's deputies are driving up now."

Lamar and the others watched as the deputies helped Thigpen from the car. Lamar thought he looked older than his seventy-five years. His aging body was bent over, and his almost bald head gleamed in the fading sunlight. The pained look on his weather-beaten face seemed to define the moment. The deputies walked slowly to accommodate Thigpen, whose weary legs looked as if they would give out.

Clicking sounds of photographers' cameras filled the air. Television news cameras rolled. Rutherford Thigpen glared defiantly and then held up a middle finger to let the reporters know what he thought of them.

"Mr. Thigpen! Mr. Thigpen," Drayton called out, pushing closer. "Why did you shoot Mr. Phillips? Did you feel your life was threatened?"

Other reporters hurled a barrage of questions at Thigpen, too. He ignored them all.

Drayton jockeyed among the horde that followed the deputies and Thigpen to the entrance of the courthouse.

"Why did you shoot him, Mr. Thigpen? Can you tell us why you shot him?" Drayton wouldn't give up.

Rutherford Thigpen looked directly into the WKCU News 6 camera, then to the ground where he placed his next step, and at the camera again.

"Can you tell us why?" Drayton asked again, placing the mic near his mouth.

"No n—— gonna talk to me the way he did!" Thigpen shouted unexpectedly, his words of hate piercing the air like a knife. "Do you know who I am?! I'm Rutherford Thigpen. I come from three generations of Thigpens in this parish."

One of the deputies grabbed him firmly and ushered him through the entrance of the building.

"Well, you heard it here on WKCU News 6," the shocked reporter said, speaking to the camera again. "This is Drayton Wilkerson reporting. We'll have more on News at Ten."

"Did you hear what he *said*?"

"Yes, we heard him loud and clear, Kyra," her dad answered.

"He shot Gramps because he felt Gramps talked back to him. You can't get lower than that."

"All that hate!" Lamar's mom murmured, shaking her head. "Hatred just festered and metastasized. It could have been any Black person."

"Papa probably wasn't gonna bow down to him like the old days," Lamar's dad added. "That old racist couldn't take it. Well, he's in jail now. But I'm afraid he's gonna get leniency because of his age."

"But, Dad," Lamar wanted to know, "how could he? He just came right out and said he shot Gramps because no n—— gonna talk to him that way."

"I heard him, Lamar. I heard him."

Lamar looked at Attorney Smith. Everyone else did, too. Lamar and the family had gained a lot of respect for him during the last week. They waited for his response, his point of view. The attorney chose his words carefully.

"This arrest is just the first step," he explained. "We have to find out what the charge will be. We should know that tomorrow or the next day. I think it should be at least second-degree murder. Rutherford Thigpen didn't plan the murder. He did, however, willfully shoot Mr. Phillips. So I think second-degree murder should be considered. We'll see. It's obvious to me, too, that this qualifies as a hate crime. And those two deputies should be charged as well. Just suspending them isn't enough. They broke the law. We also have to make sure the authorities find out who set fire to that church."

"We didn't do all this protesting for nothing, did we, Mr. Smith?" asked Lamar's mom. "It seems that there is so much more to do."

"No! No!" Attorney Smith answered quickly. "Don't underestimate what we have accomplished so far. We got the wheels of justice turning. That doesn't happen often in small towns like this. Without the protest, there probably wouldn't have been an arrest. These protests put a spotlight on this case. We just have to make sure that the wheels of justice keep turning. Listen, you all have given so much of your time to ensure that there is justice for your father and grandfather. But y'all know the road to justice is long and filled with roadblocks and discrimination that has been a part of the justice system for centuries. But you gotta be encouraged. Your efforts have made a difference."

"So do we still continue to protest?" Kyra wanted to know.

"That's your call, Kyra. You and your group and Reverend Thurmond and his people. But personally, I think we can take a break for now and see what happens. You have missed days from school and after-school activities. Others have missed days from work. We can always come back when we need to. You've forced a reckoning in this town. I don't think it can go back to the way it was."

Slowly, Lamar walked away and headed to his room.

"Lamar," his father called.

"Let him go," Lamar's mom told her husband. "He probably wants to be alone."

"I guess we've had a lot to take in for one day," Mr. Smith said.

When Lamar reached his room, he wanted to view the video he had done of his grandfather at the town council meeting. But the DA still had his laptop. Instead, he pulled out his cell phone to look at the photos he had saved of his grandfather. There were some of his Gramps giving those council people a piece of his mind. He looked at each photo intently. Then he fell across the bed, tears flowing. It seemed as if there might be justice for his grandfather. But that wouldn't bring him back. He missed his Gramps.

"Are you all right?" Kyra asked, standing in the doorway of Lamar's room.

When she saw Lamar sobbing, she walked in and sat on the bed next to him. Kyra could always find words to express what she felt, and to comment on most any situation. This time, however, she struggled. At first, the words wouldn't come.

Then she nudged Lamar. "You know what I've been thinking? Let's ask Reverend Thurmond if we can set up a Black history program at church. Do you think that's a good idea? Maybe you can help me organize it."

That caught Lamar's attention. He began wiping the tears away.

"You think he would let us do that?" he asked Kyra.

"I'm sure he would," she assured him. "We just have to put it together. Are you up for it?"

"Yeah, I guess so," Lamar answered. "I'll ask kids from the middle school to come."

Lamar sat upright on the bed and thought for a moment. Then he turned to his sister. "I got so much to learn. Gramps said that the more you know about your history, about your people, the better you're prepared to deal with anything. I got a lot to learn."

"Me too. We all got a lot to learn. So why are you sitting on that bed? Let's get to it!"

"You bet," Lamar said with a glow on his face.

"And get that video camera ready," Kyra added.

CHAPTER 28

"Y'all going to the council meeting tonight, aren't you?" Lamar asked, getting his video camcorder ready to take with him.

"We told you we're going," Lamar's dad answered. "We're going to try to attend as many meetings as we can."

"Yeah, Lamar, your father and I have been talking," Lamar's mom added. "From now on, we're gonna be more involved in what's happening in Morton. Just like Papa was. We can't be Papa, but we can do our part."

"None of us can be Papa," Lamar's dad said emphatically. "None of us."

Lamar smiled. He knew his grandfather would be happy about everyone doing their part.

The town council chamber was packed when they arrived. Lamar's parents had to search to find seats. White citizens were grouped together as before, but others were scattered among the Black citizens who dominated the meeting. Television and news reporters were there, too, including Drayton Wilkerson.

"Those sheriff's deputies gonna get what they deserve, too," someone yelled out as the Phillipses took their seats.

"Yeah, we'll take to the streets again if they don't," said another.

As usual, Kyra remained in the back, while Lamar roamed the room videotaping with his camcorder, T.C. right behind him. He gave a salute to Drayton and Victor, who were also making the rounds.

"Before we call the meeting to order," Mayor Johnson told everyone, "I would like to share a few words with you. This town and this area have been through so much over the last few weeks. But I am hopeful. There is much that lies before us. Mr. Thigpen must go on trial. The two deputies must be held accountable. The culprits who set fire to Mt. Moriah Baptist Church must be apprehended. But we will continue to move forward. We have to. And I hope all of you are willing to pull together to help us do that. Hatred is an evil. We all must fight against it. Fight against it with all our might. All of us."

After the town officials discussed the items on their agenda, Mayor Johnson asked the Phillips family to come forward.

Uneasy, Lamar's parents looked at each other. Kyra and Lamar seemed fazed by the request, too.

"Please come up front," Mayor Johnson implored again after noticing the family had not moved. "All of you. This is important."

Slowly and reluctantly, Mr. and Ms. Phillips walked to the front of the chamber, followed by their children. Once there, they each stood nervously, facing their fellow citizens.

"Councilwoman Wilcox announced earlier," the mayor said, "that the town's recreation department has received a grant to upgrade our parks and recreational activities. Among our plans is the building of a community center in the south side of the town."

The good news drew cheers. "It's 'bout time," a man yelled out.

But no one paid attention to him. Something good was going to happen in Morton, and everyone was happy about that.

"Now, the reason I have asked the Phillipses to come up front," continued the mayor, "is because I want them to know, and all of you to know, that the community center will be named the Joshua D. Phillips Community Center in honor of one of our town's heroes."

Lamar's parents gasped. For once, Kyra was speechless. As the citizens of Morton rose and applauded, he started filming, planning how he would include this special honor in his documentary. He already had the title: *Joshua Phillips: A Man of His Times.*

Then Lamar remembered the first time Gramps had taken him to a council meeting. Gramps was concerned about the unpaved streets in the Black neighborhoods in Morton. Nothing had been said about that.

"Mayor Johnson," he blurted out, "what about the unpaved streets?"

His mother gave him a disapproving stare. But Mayor Johnson beamed at Lamar.

"Lamar, we're working on that, too. I think we'll have some good news at our next council meeting."

Then he looked at the citizens of Morton and said, "Joshua Phillips's legacy lives on!"

Lamar was proud that his grandfather was being recognized for his contributions to Morton. *But what would Gramps say if he was here? The best way for me to honor Gramps,* he thought, *is for me to carry on like he would. Speak up, fight for justice and make life better for others. Yeah. That's Joshua Phillips's real legacy. We will get those streets paved, and we won't stop until we get justice for Gramps.*

Don't miss Wade Hudson's revelatory and moving memoir about growing up in the South during the heart of the Civil Rights Movement.

CHAPTER 1

Civil Rights and Protests

So this is what solitary confinement is like? I asked myself, shaking my head.

There was no one else in the tiny eight-foot-by-eight-foot cell to hear me. A small sink near a toilet stood out. There were no windows. A thin mattress with a sheet and a blanket thrown over it rested on the concrete floor. There was no pillow.

I had thought the dormitory rooms on the campus of Southern University, the institution that I attended, were small. They now seemed like large suites at the Waldorf Astoria in New York City compared to this suffocating place.

I sat down on the mattress and leaned against the brick wall. I didn't know what was happening. Why had a warrant been issued for *my* arrest? I hadn't done anything illegal!

A little more than an hour earlier, I had been in a car with two friends, on our way to a grocery store. With the windows rolled down, we were enjoying the nice spring breeze that blew into the car and cooled us off. The latest R & B hits played loudly on the radio. Suddenly, a news flash interrupted our groove and caught our attention.

> Two Negro men were arrested this morning in the Scotlandville section of Baton Rouge. They have been identified as Alphonse Snedecor and Frank A. Stewart. Both men are wanted for conspiracy to murder Baton Rouge mayor Woody Dumas and a number of other city officials, authorities said. A press conference will be held later today, when more details will be disclosed. A third man identified as Wade Hudson is being sought, authorities added. Both Stewart and Hudson are leaders of SOUL, a civil rights organization with headquarters in the Scotlandville section of Baton Rouge. Snedecor, a Baton Rouge native, is also a member of the group.

No one said a word as the music began to play again. It was as if the world had stopped.

James Holden, Stewart's cousin and the owner and driver of the car we were riding in, slammed his open hand hard against the steering wheel.

"What the . . . !" He didn't finish the sentence.

"Damn! Damn! They must have picked up Frank just after we left. This is bad."

"Who else they gonna arrest?" Barbara George, the third member of our trio, asked. The fear in her voice was apparent.

I didn't say anything. Staring at nothing in particular, I began thinking about all the other young Black freedom fighters around the country who had been arrested or killed. I had even donated to fundraising efforts for many of them. I thought about Fred Hampton and Mark Clark, Black Panther leaders who had been killed a few months earlier by the police in Chicago. Would Frank, Alphonse, or I become three more casualties?

"Holden! Take me to the bus station," I blurted. "I gotta get out of Dodge, man! I gotta get out of town. These folks will either kill me or send me to prison for the rest of my life. I got to get out of here!"

Holden pulled over to the side of the road and stopped the car. He and Barbara looked at me.

"That's what you want to do?" Holden asked pointedly.

"Yeah, man, I'm splitting! These are crazy White folks! I don't know what they'll do. You heard what the man said on the radio. They're accusing us of trying to kill the mayor and some other White officials."

"But you can't go to the bus station," Barbara interjected. "Cops are probably there, too, and at the airport."

"Well, drop me off at the bus station in Cheneyville or some other town not too far from here. I ain't going to jail for the rest of my life!"

I looked around, now concerned that the police might be closing in on us.

"Wade, if you run and they catch up with you, they'll shoot you. I'm telling you. They'll shoot you."